8-12

NOW PLAYING
STONER & SPAZ II

NOW PLAYING
STONER & SPAZ II

RON KOERTGE

CANDLEWICK PRESS

Copyright © 2011 by Ron Koertge

First edition 2011

Library of Congress Cataloging-in-Publication Data

Koertge, Ronald.

Now playing : Stoner & Spaz II / Ron Koertge — 1st ed.

p.   cm.

Sequel to: Stoner & Spaz.

Summary: High schooler Ben Bancroft, a budding filmmaker with cerebral palsy, struggles to understand his relationship with drug-addict Colleen while he explores a new friendship with A.J., who shares his obsession with movies and makes a good impression on Ben's grandmother.

ISBN 978-0-7636-5081-0

[1. Cerebral palsy — Fiction. 2. People with disabilities — Fiction.
3. Dating (Social customs) — Fiction. 4. Self-acceptance — Fiction.
5. Drug abuse — Fiction. 6. High schools — Fiction.
7. Schools — Fiction. 8. Video recordings — Fiction.]   I. Title.

PZ7.K8187Now 2011

[Fic] — dc22   2010040151

11 12 13 14 15 16 BVG 10 9 8 7 6 5 4 3 2 1

Printed in Berryville, VA, U.S.A.

This book was typeset in Perpetua.

Candlewick Press
99 Dover Street
Somerville, Massachusetts 02144

visit us at www.candlewick.com

After Stoner & Spaz *came out a few years ago, my friend Lou kept seeing Colleen everywhere. I wasn't thinking of writing a sequel, but Lou said she was sure Colleen and Ben weren't finished with me. Turns out she was right.*

I went to the movies hoping that just once
somebody would see beneath the bandages
and stitches to the huge, borrowed heart
and choose it.

I DON'T EVEN GET OUT OF BED before I light my first cigarette of the day. Light oozes through the louvered windows. Mexican light. It's already hot. A faucet squeaks in the bathroom. The woman I was sent to find is in the shower. Water like silver moonlight pouring off her body. Well, I found her all right. I found her and I'm not taking her back to the United States or the Divided States or any other states. I'm taking her somewhere nobody can find us, ever.

"Benjamin?"

"What, Grandma?"

"Are you awake?"

I can hear her right outside my door now.

"I'm going to yoga," she says. "Will you be all right?"

"You go five times a week, and when you come back, I'm always right here in one badly assembled piece."

I listen to her pad away. I've perfected getting out of bed, but it's still not easy. Thanks to cerebral palsy (aka C.P.), I'm pretty much half a kid. The right side is fine, the left not so good. I saw a tree once that'd been struck by lightning. Part of it was all shriveled up. The limbs were naked and gnarled. The other part was green and good to go. I'm that tree. Struck by lightning.

No wonder I want to be Robert Mitchum: big, strong, super-cool, with those Freon eyes of his. That's who I was pretending to be a minute ago — Robert Mitchum in *Out of the Past*.

But this is the present, where it takes me forever to get cleaned up, partly because I can't stand to look at my naked self. That's why I keep the TV on pretty much constantly. About a dozen physical therapists have told me to make friends with my body, but I just can't.

Waiting for me in the kitchen is green tea and All-Bran. Grandma thinks there'd be world peace if everybody had regular bowel movements. Colleen and I cracked each other up once talking about the global power brokers meeting in their pajamas and passing the high-fiber cereal around while they chatted amicably. *The West Bank? It's yours. Just make sure there's an ATM. Pass the prunes, okay?*

Colleen. Somebody I can't think about. So once I've choked down the last bite of bran, I cross the street to my friend Marcie's. It's early and the neighborhood is quiet except for a gardener or two. One of them is sweeping with a big push broom because there's a city ordinance about mowers or leaf blowers before eight a.m. South Pasadena is like that.

I'd be glad to push a broom if I could have two arms and two legs that worked. That's what I tell Marcie right after she answers the door.

"Really?" she says, stepping back so I can get past.

"Absolutely. I'd have a pickup truck and a bunch of clients. I'd mow and rake all day, then go home and watch DVDs."

"You should talk to them. Make another documentary."

"About gardeners?"

"Why not? Your movie about high school killed the other night." She points to the coffeepot. "Want some?"

I shake my head. "Grandma says I'm not old enough yet. And, anyway, it makes me jumpy."

Marcie sits down beside me. The caftan she's wearing this morning is blue, with gold birds on the sleeves. Her face is all angles but not hard-looking. Her life seems pretty sweet — nice house, enough money, time to do whatever she wants. But she's had heart bypass surgery, a couple of divorces, and she goes to AA meetings.

"So you're a bona fide storyteller now," she says. "Part of a community of storytellers. What's your next story? I think you ought to have a plan." She stands up before I can argue.

Marcie takes batter out of her refrigerator and starts pouring perfect little circles on the griddle.

I get down a couple of plates, the ones she made when she was a potter and had a kiln of her own and a husband. On the bottom of each plate is a line from a poem, hers for all I know. The one I'm holding says, *Pleasure is permitted me.*

"What happened to Colleen, anyway?" she asks. "She sure disappeared in a hurry."

I sit down heavily. Like there's any other way for me. "With Nick."

Marcie turns away from the stove and points a spatula at me. "And this Nick is . . . ?"

"Just a guy with a couple of joints and a Pontiac Firebird. Can we not talk about it?"

"I thought she was going to twelve-step meetings."

"She said she wasn't having any fun. I said, 'How much fun was it flat on your back in the hospital with IVs in your arm?' And she said, 'It's just a little weed this time.' How could she do that? Drive down there with us and then go home with somebody else?"

Marcie puts pancakes on my plate, then nudges the maple syrup my way.

"Besides being a card-carrying stoner, do you think she was jealous? People loved *High School Confidential.* So there you are with everybody shaking your hand, and there she is with a pin in her nose."

"Everybody didn't shake my hand, and she doesn't actually have a pin in her nose."

"I know you like her, Ben. And I'm not going to tell you girls are like buses and there'll be a new one along in a minute. But you're a talented filmmaker. You proved that at the Centrist Gallery. Concentrate on that."

I take a bite of pancake. Colleen eats at McDonald's. I've sat with her. I've paid for her coffee and McSkillet Burrito, first when she was groggy and wasted and couldn't remember the night before, and then in rehab when she couldn't shut up.

Never again, man. I'm not doing that ever again.

Marcie points her fork at me. "I've been thinking — for your next project, you need a camera of your own. You're welcome to use mine again, but it's from the Dark Ages. I'll look around online."

"Who's going to pay for it?"

"Your grandma."

I just look at her. "Grandma wants me to major in business, not film."

"You can major in business and still make movies. You don't have to be one thing; you can be a lot of things. Right now you're in high school, so you're really majoring in Getting Out with Your Frontal Lobe Intact. Anyway, all you really need is a nice little Flip Mino HD. Couple hundred bucks. Peanuts to somebody like Mrs. B."

"I don't know, Marcie."

"Tell her you'll never see Colleen again."

"Colleen's already history."

"Maybe. But your grandmother doesn't know that. And don't say, 'Oh, she was was at the gallery the other night, so she knows,' because, yes, she was there, but she wasn't thinking about Colleen." Marcie narrows her eyes. "Negotiate, Benjamin. No Colleen, all As, and merit badges in Archery and Lifesaving."

"Interesting sequence, given my skill with the bow and arrow."

"You know what I mean."

"I do. I'll ask her. I will. At the gallery, she said she was proud of me."

Marcie takes a sip of coffee. "For what it's worth, I'm not so sure Colleen's an ex-girlfriend. She likes you. I can see it when you guys are together."

"Well, she's sure got a funny way of showing it."

Marcie picks up the small remote and aims it at the little flat-screen Sony. "Let's see what's on the movie channel."

I take the bus to school. Not a regular school bus, not even the little bus, but a city bus, with real people going to real jobs. Or coming from real jobs, maybe, because about a third of my fellow passengers are crashed against the window or each other. If I had a little digital camera,

I could take pictures of people sleeping. All kinds of people. Work up some kind of montage.

I look out the window. I look with intent. Kids walking to school, hoping they're finally wearing the right outfit; people in their cars, putting on makeup, talking on their cells and eating bagels.

As we make the turn onto Glenarm, somebody's lawn sprinklers are all out of whack. A big old geyser waters the concrete, and rich guys in their BMWs and Mercedes-Benzes weave around the downpour.

Yesterday, Marcie and I watched part of *Chinatown,* Roman Polanski's great neo-noir thriller. It covers the whole William Mulholland / Owens Valley water scandal better than any history book I ever read. Without the aqueduct, L.A. would still be what the Chumash called it: "The valley of smoke." And the pollution then wasn't smog from cars and trucks, just smoke from their campfires.

I look at the buildings and the cars and the busy streets. It's hard to believe people lived in tents and adobe shacks and walked around in moccasins and hunted and fished. Nobody went to an office or to school.

There was C.P. then, too, I'll bet. There's always bad stuff. What happened to a Chumash kid with C.P.? Did he sit around with the women and bitch about the maize?

In grade school, I did a report once on the Chumash,

and they were hard-core about manhood. A kid gets to be fourteen or so, and it's time for "fasting, hallucinogenic rituals, and trials of endurance." And that last one means — I'm not kidding — lying on anthills. Anthills populated by red ants. Those big mothers.

The funny thing is, I could do that. Maybe, anyway. Probably. I've been through more than most kids, and I didn't wimp out. Ever. Hospitals, tests, physical therapy, all of it.

So I could probably lie there while the ants bit me and some shaman chanted about the seven giants that held up the world, but when I got up, I'd limp. Courageous but crippled. The really cool guys would get the Minnie Ha Ha girls, with their little fringed skirts, and I'd get Moody Boo Hoo, Minnie's bipolar sister.

Unless I could sit with the elders, the Old Ones, and listen. Native Americans have great origin myths. There are Sky Fathers and Earth Mothers and Grandmother Spiders. There are Rainbow Serpents and moon goddesses.

I'll bet I could've been that kind of storyteller then, the way Marcie says I'm the kind of storyteller I am now. The kind with a camera and a computer. I don't have to run fast or shoot straight to tell stories. I can do it sitting down.

At school, I can't help myself. I look for Colleen. I want to see her and I don't want to see her. I want to talk to her and I don't. I want her to be sorry she took off with that guy, and if she is, it'll just make me mad because she can never be sorry enough.

I sit through history and social studies, then hobble down to eat lunch. Colleen almost never eats at school. She and Ed used to climb in his car, fire up a joint, then inhale four orders of onion rings at Wolfies. And she still had beautiful skin. Once when we were alone at Marcie's, she took off all her—

"Hey, man."

It's Reshay Pettiford. He's about six three, wearing a Kobe tank top two hundred times too big for him.

I step away from the big double doors that lead into the cafeteria and the usual lemming suicide stampede. "What's up?" I ask.

"I want you to put me in your movie. You talked to Debra. You got her side the story. I want you to get my side. She come on to me. She was all, 'You don't have to worry. It's taken care of.' And the next thing I know, it's, 'You my baby daddy. You got to do the right thing.' You know what I mean, little man. She's like that Colleen. She'd go with anybody."

"Colleen's not that way. She won't go with just anybody."

"She went with you."

"And I'm what? The bottom of the barrel?"

"I'm just saying."

I look hard at him. He's either been shooting hoops or he's scared to death, because he's dripping sweat. He's not Native American, but I can guess his origin myth: the earth was without form and void until Phil Jackson came along with the triangle defense and covered part of the earth with highly polished maple.

"The movie you're talking about is kind of done," I tell him. "It opened at eight p.m. and closed at ten."

He grimaces. "Dang. I'll bet it don't make me look good."

"You can see it if you want."

He shakes his head. "That's all right. I know it make me out to be the fool." He wipes his face by pulling up the tank top and using it like a towel. "You gonna do another one?" he asks. "Let everybody else testify?"

I nod. "We'll see, okay?" That's an answer I learned from my grandma. It always means there's no way.

He holds out one fist and I tap it with my good hand. Everybody's afraid of the other one. Everybody except Colleen.

"Let me have my say when you do, awright?"

He's through with me then and charges through the doors and heads right for his homies. Somebody whips a basketball to him at what looks to me like almost the speed of light. Reshay charges, dribbling low and hard a couple of times, making tricky moves, ball between his legs, head fake — the whole NBA tryouts package, and right in the corner of the school cafeteria.

To be able to do that. To be agile and dexterous.

I look for an empty table. There are my classmates: Preppy, Sporty, Goth, Emo, Skater, Mansonite, Mean Girl (aka Heather, from *Heathers,* a Michael Lehmann movie I've seen about six times).

"So, am I famous yet?"

I turn around and there's Oliver Atkins, looking like he just stepped out of a Banana Republic ad. As usual.

I tell him, "You missed it."

He points, so I take a cafeteria tray and shuffle forward while he says, "Why don't you dice and slice that little movie of yours and put the best parts on YouTube."

"And your part would be the best part, right?"

"One of, anyway."

Right in front of me is something in a big pan that looks like curds and whey. I point and wait for the lady in the hairnet to hand it over.

That's when I see Colleen. She's wearing a flimsy little dress and trashed motorcycle boots with the laces undone. She's not lining up for lunch, either. She's looking around.

I tell Oliver good-bye, put my head down, pay for my lunch, scuttle toward an empty corner, and pretend to eat. I try to act surprised when she sits across from me.

Her skin is see-through pale, and everything just stands still for a second.

She says, "I thought I'd test the limits of the word *tardy*."

I glance at my watch and pretend to be casual. "So far, so good."

"What were you talking to Reshay about?"

I shrug. "He wants his say if I ever make another documentary."

"So you'd what? Follow him around with a camera? I can tell you how that's going to come out. He'll go to some community college on a little scholarship, flunk out, then come back here and get in trouble."

I pick at my lunch. Colleen reaches across, takes a little bit between her fingers, inspects it, puts it back.

"Hey," I tell her. "Go handle your own lunch."

"Why don't we cut to the chase here, Ben. How mad are you? And put that fork down before you answer."

I take a deep breath. "I had to tell my grandma that you had a headache, so your mom picked you up."

That seems to push her away from the table. "You should switch from documentaries to sci-fi. In what parallel and much more attractive universe would my mother ever pick me up from anywhere?"

"Do you still mean what you said about getting high every now and then?"

She shakes her head. Or maybe moves it ambiguously.

"I wouldn't pay too much attention to anything I say when I'm buzzed."

We sit for a minute. She always wears this patchouli stuff, and the scent wafts over my mac and cheese. Queen Victoria used patchouli in her linen chests. And how do I know that? Because I Googled everything about Colleen, including the stuff she dabs behind her ears. And other places. Why is that any more pathetic than watching seven movies a day?

I can't look directly at her. I focus on her hands — the gnawed cuticles, the black, chipped nail polish. I poke at my ice cream, which is still as hard as a meteorite. "What now?" I ask.

"Well, that's easy. Now I go to a meeting, say, 'Hello, I'm Stupid and I've been clean for forty-eight hours.' What about you?"

I shake my head and say, "I don't know."

"Want to do something after school? Get something to eat, go to a movie, fool around?" She stands up. "I know what. Let's go to your house. I love your room. It's unbelievably tidy. How do you do that? I tried dusting once and I hated it. I mean, what's the point? It's just dusty again tomorrow."

I know she wants something, and I don't care. I'm just glad to see her again. I'm not addicted to drugs, like she is; I'm addicted to her.

I ask. "You seem a little amped."

13

She shakes her head. "Caffeine. Not like you mean. So, what do you think?" She points out the window, toward that other world. "Want to get out of here?"

"I've got class, Colleen."

"After, then? I need to talk to you about something."

Ah, here it comes. "Give me a hint?"

"Are you sure you don't want to go to your house? I might have to take a shower. You might have to bring me a towel."

"How many pages?"

She grins and her teeth seem pointier. "Just three. On Ralph Waldo Emerson's 'Over-Soul.'"

I stand up first. "Well, I'll tell you what. Because we had such a good time at the gallery the other night, because going to dinner afterward with you and my grandma and Marcie was so much fun, I'll absolutely help you write your paper."

"I'm sorry, okay? I made a mistake."

I put my tray down. "What a crappy thing to do, Colleen. How could—?" But that's as far as I get before she goes off on me.

"One 'I'm sorry' is all you get from me, pal. I apologize, you accept, we move on. That's it. No lectures, no whining, no raking over the smoldering coals."

"Well, then maybe you should do your paper by yourself, because I'm still mad."

"Fine. And maybe you should jerk yourself off with your one functioning hand."

I can't stomp off in a huff, so I leave that move to her. I just take my tray to the big aluminum racks. On the way, though, I pass Chana and Molly, girls I interviewed for *High School Confidential*.

Molly shakes her finger at me. "You better off without her, Gimpalong."

I sit through two more classes, I take notes dutifully, I remember to remember the main points. If the teacher calls on me, I answer. Then at three thirty, when school is officially out, I make my way to the parking lot and lean on Colleen's Volkswagen. The one Ed bought her with money made selling weed.

I don't quite know what I'll do if she shows up with Ed or somebody who wants to buy weed or even a girlfriend from detention, but when I spot her, she's alone. She sees me, too, from kind of a long way off, and she raises one hand. So I wave back.

"Lots of Sturm und Drang, huh?" She puts one hand up and rubs my cheek, and just like that I'm hers. I was, anyway.

I ask, "Did you know that Donder and Blizten mean *thunder* and *lightning*?"

"Santa's reindeer? No fucking way!"

"Yeah. Dasher and Dancer and Prancer and Vixen and Thunder and Lightning."

"When I was little, my mom told me Rudolph's nose was red from heavy drinking."

I reach for her dress and pull her toward me. "So there's jolly old Saint Nick, but his main reindeer was alcoholic?"

She leans into me. "Is that a three-page essay on Emerson in your pocket, or are you just happy to see me?"

I let myself put my arms . . . well, my arm, around her. "I'm not even sure Mae West said that line, but if she did, it was in *Sextette*."

"Can we go to your house?"

I shake my head. "Grandma's home."

"Want to just make out in the backseat like people did before rock and roll all but eliminated Judeo-Christian civilization as we know it?"

I could just do this forever. Stand by her car, feel her against me, say anything.

I whisper, "You know, 'Give somebody a fish and she eats once. Teach her to fish and she eats forever.'"

"So that's a fish in your pocket?"

"I'm saying we should work on your paper. But instead of writing it for you, I'll show you what to do so you can write any paper anytime."

She leans in a little more and puts her face against

mine. "You sound like some guy on television who's about to throw in a second ShamWow! if I order in the next ten minutes."

I don't care if she really likes me or not. All I care about is that she's doing what she's doing. Doing it to me. Ben the loser recluse. Ben the spaz.

"That's the deal," I say. "Take it or leave it."

She kisses me quick and hard, finds the keys in her purse, hops in her little convertible without bothering with the door, and looks up at me. "So what are you waiting for? Are you going to teach me to fish or not?"

Colleen likes Buster's, this cool little coffee shop in South Pasadena, which is, for the record, not just southern Pasadena but a whole other city. Pretty and green. Pricey. We'll end up sitting outside just a block or so from a store that sells seven-hundred-dollar baby strollers. I know because Grandma and her yoga friends chipped in and bought one for someone in their morning class.

Colleen drives us south. We stand in a little line and order from Ayanna with the butterfly tattoo on her shoulder and the pierced lip. I've got the money and I order what Colleen likes (caramel macchiato), but the barista looks at Colleen. It's not flirty or anything like that; they're birds of a feather and I'm not.

Have I ever connected with anybody like that, ever?

Amy, maybe. A little, anyway. She was in the Centrist Gallery show, too. She wants to go to film school, and she gave me her e-mail address.

Colleen and I settle into a table under the green awning. Well, she settles; I brace myself and sink. The bracing isn't pretty, but I've tried just sitting down, got all tangled up in myself, and ended up flat on my back like a turtle, wishing somebody would just turn me over and let me crawl into the desert and die.

She takes my good hand between both of hers and rubs it briskly. "You okay, Ben? You're cold."

"Just thinking about Emerson."

Colleen pretends to shudder. "Makes me cold all over." She sips her drink, nods at a skate punk who checks her out as he hurtles by, then scrutinizes a couple of nannies who cruise up, speaking nonstop Spanish.

They park their strollers, and the angel-haired toddlers hold up their perfect arms.

Colleen points at the kids. *"Lindo. Lindos niños."*

The nannies nod and smile, then go inside.

I tell her, "I didn't know you spoke Spanish."

She shakes her head. "I don't. I know, like, ten words. Ed's pretty good, actually. The smugglers like it when you use their native tongue."

"Do you ever want kids?" I ask.

"Get serious. Do you?"

"Are you kidding?"

She takes a drink from her tall glass, wipes the foam off her lip with an index finger, then licks that. "Why 'Are you kidding?' You don't have C.P. where it counts; we know that. And you've got money to burn. You could marry somebody nice and have all the kids you want."

"Let's talk about Ralph."

"Who?"

"Ralph Waldo Emerson."

"Oh, yeah. Him. You never think about anybody talking to these, like, icons and calling them by their first names. 'Ralph, either put on those Over-Souls or you can't go out and play with Thoreau!'"

Colleen has a terrific laugh. High but not screechy. Big but not booming. Robust, I guess. For a girl, anyway. Especially one who weighs about ninety-two pounds.

I ask, "What's the assignment, exactly?"

"Compare Emerson's belief system with three or four others."

"So it's just research."

She sits back in a semi-huff. "Fine. I'll do it myself." She runs her hand up my arm. "I just thought if you loved me, you'd do it for me."

"Nice try."

"Love is bullshit, anyway," she says. "But you like me, right? Like hanging out with me?"

"I can take it or leave it."

She's out of her chair, leaning over the table, kissing me, asking, "Really?"

I wait till I can breathe again before I say, "So I'd rather take it."

People stare at us, or at her, maybe. Are they thinking, *How can she do that to a gimp like him?* Or do they just think, *Get a room?* The guys can't take their eyes off Colleen: that incredible skin, the in-your-face tats, the lazy way she smokes, the bitter curve of her lips. One of them — his wife keeps barking orders: "Get some napkins," "Get some more milk," "Pick up one of the twins, no not that one, the other one" — probably sees her just like I do, she's the gatekeeper to another world. Like in the ads for movies: *A world of danger, intrigue, desire. A world where almost everything is a mistake.*

When he won't stop staring, I glare at him and ask, "What?"

He looks down, embarrassed, and I feel the rush of testosterone.

Colleen does a pretty good imitation of De Niro in *Taxi Driver*. "Are you lookin' at me?" Which makes me blush.

There's that laugh of hers again, big but weirdly like wind chimes, too. "You are so cute," she says.

Then we sit for a little while. Young parents cruise by, a homeless guy with a Santa pack of recyclables over one shoulder, another nanny or two chatting on cell phones to some humid country I only know about from coloring it green in the second grade.

I could sit all afternoon and just be with her, but Colleen gets restless. I know we're just about to get up when a couple of women walk by. They're just in shorts and T-shirts and flip-flops. But their shorts are shorter, their T-shirts are tighter, and they're put together in a way even the yoga moms aren't. One of them—short, rice-white hair and a snake tattoo winding up one calf—stops.

"Colleen? What are you doing here?"

"Hey!" Colleen stands up and they hug. Then she points to me. "I'm just hanging out with my pal Constantinopolous, the Greek shipping tycoon. He's got so much gold in those cargo pants, he can't stand up, so he's not just being rude."

"Ben," I say, holding out my good hand. "Don't pay any attention to her."

"Who are you guys these days?" Colleen asks.

The tattooed one says, "Uh, I think I'm Tawny, and she's Crystal."

Crystal elbows her friend. "It's Amber, dumb ass." Then they both laugh.

"Want to sit?" Colleen asks.

They shake their heads. "We gotta go."

We watch them—everybody watches them—get

into a blue Miata convertible and zoom away. I wait and see. Colleen will either tell me or she won't.

"There's something you ought to know," she says after a very long minute or two. "I mean, it's no big deal, but better you hear it from me than some vindictive bitch at school who wants you all to herself."

She doesn't mean it, that last part, but I like to hear it. "Okay. Whenever you're ready."

She takes a deep breath. "Those girls are strippers. They change their names every time they work at a new club. There's this kind of, you know, crop rotation, so customers don't have to look at the same boob jobs all the time."

"Do you know their real names?"

She shakes her head. "I'm not sure they do anymore. The one with all the collagen used to be a Mormon. 'Let's hear it for the beautiful Hulga from Salt Lake City,' right? No way. So it's Raven or Peaches or Toffee or Dawn."

I just nod. This is her narrative.

"Um, well, let's just cut to the chase here: my mom's a stripper, too, okay? She works downtown at this club called Girls Before Swine."

"I thought you said your mom was a waitress."

Colleen squirms. "Well, she waits for guys to stuff twenties in her thong. I probably should have told you before."

"So I know now. No big deal."

She looks at me, one eye half closed suspiciously. "'No big deal.' Is that it?"

"I don't know what you want me to say. Your mom's an exotic dancer. Mine's a missing person. I'd rather have yours."

"It doesn't matter to you?"

"I don't think so. Does it matter to you?"

She takes a deep breath. "Ed hated it."

"No way. Ed's an entry-level felon. What's he doing judging — ?"

"Ed's a chauvinist dickhead. He thinks women ought to stay home."

"You were his girlfriend."

"I was a toy, okay? He played with me."

"You told me you carried dope in your underpants so he wouldn't get caught with it."

"So I was a toy mule. This isn't about Ed and me; it's about my mom."

"Colleen, I don't care what your mom does for a living. I'm glad she doesn't torture small animals for minimum wage, but except for that —"

She blurts, "Kids made fun of me."

I push her coffee toward her and she takes one last sip, then makes a face. I ask, "What kids?"

"Kids at school. When they found out, it was fucking awful."

I take her hand. "C'mon, you know how kids are.

They're hyenas. They harass the weak and the wounded until they collapse, and then they eat them. When I was in grade school, some jerk found out my mom ran away from home. He told everybody. First, I was one of the untouchables, anyway, because of the C.P. Then I'm so toxic my mom can't stand me, and then after school my grandma pulls up in that Cadillac. Pity and envy are a nasty combination. If you ever have to mix them in chemistry, wear protective goggles."

"They called her a whore. I'm nine years old. What am I supposed to do with that except punch their lights out?"

"I wish I'd punched everybody's lights out instead of hiding in the Rialto."

"At least you know a lot about movies. What do I know except names for weed? Angola, baby bhang, Canadian black, Don Juan—"

"Yeah, but look how nicely you alphabetize them."

She can't help but laugh as she picks up my good hand, pulls it to her, and kisses it. "I missed you."

"Really? Then I'll tell you what. Go with Grandma and me and probably Marcie to this concert Saturday night, and I'll write that Emerson essay for you."

THIS OUGHT TO BE INTERESTING. Colleen at the Norton Simon Museum. And not just wandering around looking at paintings, but sitting down in one of the galleries and listening to chamber music. Well, at least there won't be some tall guy outside with a muscle car and some hemp rolling papers.

I'm ready to go: brick-colored J. Crew khakis, one of their cotton/cashmere sweaters, and some cool shoes called Planet Walkers that slip right on. Colleen picked out the sweater and likes the shoes. She said to the salesman, "My boyfriend here would really like the Planet Lurchers so he can emphasize his disability and everybody will feel sorry for him, but he'll settle for the Walkers."

I liked being called her boyfriend.

I'm leaning in the door of my grandma's bedroom while she puts on a few diamonds. She knows some high-end jewelers downtown, the kind with a guard at the door and a space-station air-lock entrance. She owns one of those loupes, those eyepieces, and she and Mr. Biddle take turns looking through it while they diss the new, callow rich. The upstarts and Powerball winners who come in and buy the biggest thing in the display case. Grandma's old-school. She and Mr. Biddle agree that they are from an era when the word *elegant* meant something.

She's got one photo on her dresser, and that's of her and my grandfather. In a bad movie, right now there'd be this montage where that photo melted into one of my parents and me, and that one turned into just my parents, et cetera.

My grandma would never be in a bad movie. My father's dead, and that's that; photographs would just remind her. And Mom? I guess she was kind of a basket case. I kind of remember her and I kind of don't.

She turns around. "How do I look?"

My grandma likes linen and silk. She shops where everybody knows her name. They call her when new stuff comes in. The next day, she sits and sips bottled water while they show her things.

I tell her, "You always look good."

"Someday, Benjamin," she says, "you're going to have to take care of our assets."

"What happened to Flatterum, Leechum, and Bill-umtilltheysqueal?"

"There are family matters to be taken into consideration."

"Right. They're family lawyers."

She puts her hand up to my face. Her skin is warm and dry. "We need to talk soon, dear."

"What about?"

We both look up at the sound of the doorbell, and I say that I'll get it.

When I open the door, Marcie points at Colleen and

says, "Look who I bumped into on your lawn. What a coincidence!"

They both kiss me, and Marcie says how nice I look. She's ready for a short hike, in cargo pants and crewneck, and Colleen has her B-girl look down (sideways baseball cap, tight black pants but not so tight she couldn't bust a few moves if she wanted to, tank top with *Floor Angelz* on it, sneaks).

Grandma makes her usual entrance. "Hello, everyone."

Colleen mutters, "Your Highness. I bring news from Paris that I hope will not distress you. It's about the dauphin's hernia." But immediately she goes right up to Grandma and says, "I'm sorry about last week at that gallery. I should have come in and said good-bye, headache or no headache. I didn't mean to be rude."

"Thank you, dear. Apology accepted." She checks her watch. "Probably we should go. The concert is at seven, and there are no reserved seats."

We follow her toward the garage. Marcie and Grandma talk about roses. Marcie actually gardens. Grandma goes out with a sixty-dollar basket from Pottery Barn and her Felco forged-steel pruning shears and has the gardener hold the bush steady for her while she clips.

Colleen whispers, "Where are we going again?"

"The Norton Simon Museum. Chamber music in the north gallery."

"Probably not going to be a mosh pit, huh?"

"If there is, let's try and keep Grandma out of it. You know how she gets when she hears 'I Wanna Be Sedated.'"

The three of us stand on the sidewalk while the car oozes out of the garage. Marcie gets in front, Colleen and me in the back.

Grandma gets to the end of the driveway, then waits until the street is completely empty in both directions, maybe as far as the Atlantic and the Pacific.

I ask Colleen, "Everything okay?"

She warns me, "Don't check on me every two seconds. I'm fine."

I settle back into the leather. I shouldn't have said anything. When I was little, Grandma used to constantly ask me how I felt, and it was a real drag. So I spend a little time wondering what Grandma wants to talk to me about "soon." What is it that a lawyer can't handle and I can?

We're somewhere on Orange Grove Boulevard, maybe halfway to the museum, when Colleen whispers, "Good thing Ed's not back here. He'd cut Grandma's ears off to get at those diamonds."

"Where is Ed, anyway? I haven't seen him at school."

She shakes her head. "Boot camp. He got busted, and the cop said, 'The army or we go up in front of a judge.' But I really don't care where he is. When I go to meetings, some chick is always saying how she ran into this dude from before, and the next thing she knows, she's high again. I know what she means. I can't be around Ed or anybody else like that. That's why I like you. All you're going to turn me on to is mango sorbet."

"Can I ask you about something else? Do you think your mom would talk to me about her work?"

"'Her work.' She slithers up and down a pole and takes her clothes off."

"I'm thinking about making another documentary. I've got a new camera. Marcie talked Grandma into buying it for me. It's really cool. Super-sharp, sound, the whole nine yards. Check this out." I open the satchel Colleen and I bought one day at Old Navy and show her.

She looks through the little viewfinder. "Sounds like you just want to take pictures of naked girls."

I shake my head. "I want to talk to the girls who get naked. Working in clubs is a whole other world, okay? It's got to have rules and rites and all that stuff, just like high school. Like, how old can you be before you're kicked out of the tribe? What's the shoptalk like? Are the girls saving to go to college, or do they spend money as fast as they get it? There's got to be, like, a thousand stories just in their dressing room."

She leans closer, so she's almost whispering. Her breath is warm and I can smell the patchouli. "If it's stories you want, try this one: My mom knows this chick who lived with a schoolteacher, okay? Sweet guy. Taught third grade. Liked to cook. So, she comes home at two thirty a.m. with her little stripper purse full of ten-dollar bills, and he's there with, like, lentil loaf and a glass of carrot juice. He's been doing lesson plans, and there's all these little maps and shit from his kids who adore him. I mean, she's seen these kids, okay, gone to some play where they're all dressed like dairy products or something."

"How'd they even meet?"

"Supermarket. Some guy recognized her and wouldn't leave her alone, so Mr. Super Teacher steps in. Chicks love that Sir Galahad shit."

"This story isn't going to have a happy ending, is it?"

She shakes her head. "Six months or so later, she takes up with some hard-core scumbag from the club."

"Wow."

"No kidding."

Grandma turns off Colorado and into the parking lot. She says something to the nearest guard, who walks over and moves a big safety cone that had been guarding a primo parking spot.

Without being asked, Grandma says, "I called ahead. I'm on the board."

Colleen whispers, "Unfuckingbelievable."

We stroll up the steps and past the first of about two thousand guards. Grandma points to this big, black sculpture of six bronze guys and says in her docent's voice,

"*The Burghers of Calais.* It's actually quite a lovely story. The English had cut off the town of Calais, and people were dying. Months with almost no food and very little water. So the richest men in town got together and gave themselves up as hostages. That way the others would survive. They're dressed in those loose clothes because what they had on was basically their underwear or their pajamas. They didn't want to go over to the English in their finery because they knew they'd be killed for sure."

"So were they?" Colleen asks.

Grandma shakes her head. "King Edward's wife, Philippa, was pregnant and, luckily for the mayor of Calais and his friends, superstitious. She thought it would be bad luck for her unborn child."

Inside, Grandma and Marcie show their membership cards. Colleen takes in the scene: sculptures and paintings, busts and bronzes. And not all crammed together, either. The place is huge.

I've been here a lot. When I was little, Grandma would drive up all the time and "expose me to art." Like art was some kind of dandy virus I'd be lucky to catch.

Colleen shudders. "I'd hate to polish these floors, I'll tell you that."

"Now, there's an idea for a documentary," I tell her. "If just being around great art is good for a person, are the janitors here happier than the average maintenance men?"

She pulls me toward the nearest guard, a guy in his twenties with a wispy mustache.

"Can I ask you something?" she says. "You're here every day, right? Do you feel different when you go home?"

He looks at us both before he answers. "My feet hurt."

"So art doesn't, like, seep into your pores or anything."

He shrugs. "It's just a job."

As we make our way back to Marcie and Grandma, I tell Colleen, "Except he's not the only guy in his father's white shirt and a blue blazer that doesn't fit."

She asks, "How do you and your little camera ever get people to tell the whole truth and nothing but the truth, anyway?"

"When I did that thing at school for the show at that gallery, it just took time. I mean, for every minute I could use, I probably talked to our beloved classmates for an hour."

"It sounds like *Wild Kingdom,* you know? You lay there in the bushes forever just to finally catch a warthog taking a crap."

"Making a documentary is totally like *Wild Kingdom.* You wait and you wait and you listen and you ask and then you have to be lucky. Like, I know there's at least one guard here who'd say he's kinder or more patient or happier or something just from being around all this beautiful stuff."

"Well, I don't feel a whole lot happier. This place gives me a headache." She points to a portrait. Some nobleman with a huge wig and a simper. She drags me closer. "Painting's hard—I get that. All the little hairs, the sun off his gold buttons. But why him? He's probably humping the downstairs maid while his wife's upstairs with her insides falling out from having one kid after another. Where's his wife's picture, huh? Or where's the cook and the girl who does the laundry?"

"They can't afford to have somebody paint their pictures."

"Exactly! So why should I give a shit about him?"

My grandma knows a lot of people. She stops and talks to them for a minute, anyway, and introduces us over and over. All of a sudden, Colleen is having a hard time holding it together. She was okay outside and okay when we talked to that guard. Now she's not so okay. She's gone all pale and twitchy.

When I first met Colleen and started to hang with her, my grandma said she hoped I wasn't one of those men who liked to rescue women. She said Colleen was just the kind of victim to bring out that tendency in me. My father was like that, she said.

Except it was Colleen who rescued me. Took me

places I'd never have gone to on my own. Took off her clothes so I could see a real naked girl once in my life. Helped me off with mine and didn't laugh or throw up.

I go and stand beside her. I put my arm around her and pull her toward me. I feel her breathe about a hundred times a minute.

"Take it easy."

She nods. "I know. It's just a little panic attack. No big deal."

The concert is at the end of a long gallery on the east side of the building. A hundred and fifty fold-ing chairs in a semicircle. A huge painting — as big as a trampoline — right behind where the musicians will sit.

"I don't want anybody next to me," she says, holding my hand tight.

"All right. I'll tell Grandma my hip is bothering me. We'll stand by the door."

When I get back from passing around my little lie, Colleen is watching the musicians. They've been escorted in by two guards. God forbid some terrorists would cap-ture a cellist.

They're nervous, tuning their violins, fussing with their collars. Colleen hands me the program she's been reading and I glance at the bios: Juilliard. The Eastman School. First violin for the St. Louis Symphony. Winner of a Ruth Cole Webber scholarship.

Just then Grandma hurries back to whisper, "Listen carefully to the adagio in this first piece."

A minute later, the quartet passes us, and during the applause that starts at just the sight of them, Colleen says, "I have to get out of here." And she bolts.

I can't keep up, but I still follow her down the long hall, past the pears and the cheese in the still life, past the duke of something and his smug wife, past Virtue and Vice in a sixteenth-century slap-down, all the way through the big glass doors to the garden, with its huge, shadowy sculptures and shimmery pond.

I stand off to one side, watch her punch numbers, then bark into her cell phone, "I don't understand your so-called Higher Power at all, okay? What kind of Higher Power would stick me with this life? And my boyfriend limps all the time, thanks to a bad hand God dealt him. That's the God you want me to turn my life over to?"

The light is gorgeous — filtering down from big arcs on Orange Grove Boulevard, flowing out of the gallery and pooling on the crushed gravel. As Colleen paces, she kicks up a few leaves, and they somersault in her wake. *Turning over a new leaf.*

I slyly take out my camera. I don't need to use the viewfinder. I can shoot from the hip.

"I know I was wrong," Colleen says. "How many

times do I have to say it? And I harmed people. I know that drill."

I pan a little to the right. Half a dozen skinny poplar trees flank the pond. In the moonlight, the whole thing looks enchanted. It's so pretty, it's too pretty, and that's what Colleen, in her dance-hall pants, does for that scene: she rubs it the wrong way.

"No," she says. "I'm not going to use. I'm better. I just had a bad moment and you said to call. Really, I'm fine. I'm at a museum. Seriously. Thanks."

I watch her dig in her purse again, this time for a cigarette. So I walk over and remind her, "You can't smoke here."

"Are you kidding? We're outside."

I shrug.

She's holding a cigarette, which she snaps in two, and tosses it toward the water.

"This whole thing is really not my scene." She waves her arm at everything. "The best part was when we came in and Marcie was cruising those two old guys by the gift shop. But then I have to stand by those snooty violinists who remind me I've wasted my life, and then Grandma What-a-Big-Mouth-You-Have has to come back and tell me what to listen for. I wanted to wring her scrawny neck."

I tug at her. "C'mon."

"I don't want to listen to that classical shit. I want

some guy with his shirt off to scream at me and then set his guitar on fire."

"We can't do that right now, but maybe afterward, if you still want."

Then she turns to me. Or on me, maybe. "Don't be too nice to me, Ben, okay? Just don't. I know me, and I'll just end up hating your guts. Understand?"

"No."

She says, "You don't know anything, do you?" Then she steps right up to me, pulls my face toward hers, and kisses me, shoving her tongue in my mouth and holding on to me so long that a guard finally comes over and tells us to cut it out or we'll have to leave.

An hour later, I'm in my bedroom, hanging up my jacket, and wondering where Colleen went after we got back from the museum. She drove away about a hundred miles per hour. Maybe she's right and I don't know anything, but I'll bet she's on her way to get high.

Grandma knocks, then pushes the door open. She crosses the thick-as-tundra carpet, comes and stands beside me and adjusts some hangers so they're all half an inch apart. She watches her hands like they aren't hers. "Colleen never fails to upset me."

"I know. Me, too, sometimes."

"Has she asked you for money, Benjamin?"

I shake my head.

"Not even a little?"

"It's not like that."

"Well, I didn't come in here to talk about her." She wanders to my desk, lifts the ivory-colored keyboard, runs one finger under it, then looks for dust. "I came to say that I was chatting with Marcie tonight and I've decided that, in addition to the new camera, you may also have a Verizon account of your own."

That makes me get to my feet. Or try to. "All right!"

"I'll get a technician to come tomorrow afternoon. You should be here. If you have an engagement, cancel it. There may be technical things he'll want you to know."

"Thanks, Grandma. I promise I won't prowl the Internet looking for pictures of naked girls holding Roman candles."

She winces just a little. "Don't promise. Marcie says boys your age can't help themselves."

"Are you and Marcie kind of tight now?"

"She likes you a great deal. She thinks you have enormous potential." She comes over and pats me like I'm Ben the Wonder Dog. "Of course, I do, too. Your father was very, very bright."

"It's funny that's he's dead and we talk about him sometimes, but Mom's alive and we never talk about her."

"I'm willing," Grandma says. "We can talk now if you want."

I fall back on my bed. "Maybe tomorrow. I'm pretty tired."

Grandma is halfway out the door when I say, "Why do you think she left without me?"

Grandma turns. "So we're talking, after all?"

I get up to go to the bathroom. "No. Forget it. I need to brush my teeth."

Ten minutes later, I get in bed and dial Colleen one more time. She doesn't pick up. So I get to lie there in the dark and worry.

It's a long day without Colleen, who's absent again. AWOL. MIA. But at least Carlos the Verizon guy shows up right after I get back from school. It's not that hot in the San Gabriel Valley, but the weather can't seem to make up its mind, and the sky isn't exactly clear, but it's not exactly cloudy, either. Blurry, maybe.

None of it has put Carlos in a good mood, and it doesn't help when Grandma asks him if he would mind taking off his shoes. Then she points to her moonlight-colored carpet.

He follows me to my bedroom. "Your grandmother must have a lot of clout," he says. "She just called this morning."

"She always knows a guy who knows a guy."

"You're telling me. The usual wait time is two weeks." He looks the place over, then reaches into his tool belt.

He's got a panther tattoo high up on his right arm. His huge right arm.

I point. "Did that hurt?"

"Not bad. You thinking about getting one?"

"You saw my grandma, right?"

He finally looks at me and grunts. "She can't stop you when you're eighteen."

"You want a Coke or something?"

"A Coke would be great, man. I'd really appreciate it."

I meet Grandma in the kitchen, where she's just hanging up the phone. "Everything's fine," she says.

I reach all the way in the back of the fridge, where it's really cold. "Who said it wasn't?"

"Thieves with technical know-how intercept the dispatcher, arrive ahead of schedule wearing polo shirts with the appropriate logo, then hit the home owner over the head, tie her up, and rob her."

"'Thieves with technical know-how'?"

"Better safe than sorry, Benjamin." She reaches for the cold can of soda. "Let me put that in a glass."

"No way. I'm not Jeeves."

When I get back to the room, Carlos is down on his knees under the desk, so I set the can on a coaster Grandma makes me keep there. Then he gets up, pretty much collapses into my Aeron chair, and drains the Coke.

He's wearing a wedding ring, and I wonder what it's

like to work eight hours at a real job, then take two good arms and legs home to your family.

Before Colleen, if some genie had offered me Carlos's life or mine, I'd have taken his in a heartbeat. What did I do, anyway, but limp down the street to the Rialto Theatre? I spent more time in the dark than a bat.

If I had to choose now, I'm not so sure, because Colleen —

"What happened to you, anyway?" Carlos asks.

I know what he means. "C.P."

He shakes his head.

I explain, "It's, like, a birth defect."

"So you're stuck with it."

I say, "Pretty much."

"But your brain is okay."

I just nod.

He looks at my framed posters (James Dean and Jeanne Moreau). He knows I don't have to sweep the floor or clean my own bathtub. "And you've got money," he says. "That never hurts." He turns around in the chair and motions for me. I like it that he doesn't stand up and offer me a seat like I'm some poor old guy with Velcro shoelaces and expandable pants. "Let's get you online. You've probably got a lot of people you want to talk to."

Only one, actually. But I don't tell him that.

Ten minutes later, I follow Carlos to the door,

Grandma appears and signs some paperwork, he and I shake hands.

When we're alone, Grandma says, "I'm steaming broccoli, Benjamin. My yoga teacher says everyone should eat broccoli every day. Is there anything else you'd like?"

I'd like to be six-two and 180 pounds of lean muscle. Oh, and I'd like Colleen to come in and kiss me like she's never kissed anybody else, ever.

I settle for, "Maybe a baked potato?"

"That'll take a while. Is that all right?"

It's more than all right. It's exactly what I want: time to compose an e-mail to Amy, the girl I met at the Centrist Gallery. Who loves movies. Who gave me her e-mail address and made me promise I'd write, while outside, Colleen was climbing into some stranger's Firebird.

That's how it is with Colleen: I'm dying to see her and she makes me so mad. And, as far as Amy goes, I wonder if she even remembers me. She could've handed out her e-mail to everybody at that gallery.

I find the piece of paper she gave me right where I'd hidden it and start typing. I remind her who I am (Ben Bancroft), where we met (on Melrose at that gallery), and what I brought to show that night (*High School Confidential*). I tell her that I remember her documentary (*Roach Coach*). I say that it'd be fun to get together sometime when she's not busy and just hang out. Finally I hit Send. Then I lean back and take a deep breath.

Ten minutes later, while I'm looking at IFC's movie lineup, I actually have mail! My first. And it's from Amy, but it's signed *A.J.* The message is two words — *Call me* — and a phone number.

I don't even stop to think or worry about what I'm going to say. I just punch in the numbers before I lose my nerve.

"Amy? It's me. Ben Bancroft."

"Hi, Ben Bancroft. But it's A.J. I just used Amy on that documentary because I wanted people to know it was made by a girl. But everybody calls me A.J. How are you?"

"I'm good. I've got e-mail. Obviously."

"Cool. Nobody likes a Luddite."

Then there's silence. That silence. Where nobody knows exactly what to say. In the movies, couples don't just wait for each other to say something. Like, in *Notting Hill,* Hugh Grant spills orange juice on Julia Roberts. Or two people are in a store, they both want an umbrella, and there's only one left, so they fight over it. They're like sour cream and chutney, oil and water, paper and fire. Total opposites. Until their eyes meet.

It happened that way for Colleen and me at the Rialto. Dreary old me, dragging one leg, and a totally amped Colleen in a lime-green miniskirt.

"Oh," A.J. says finally. "A friend of mine got something on YouTube. It's just his Rottweiler playing the *Reservoir Dogs* video game, but it's kind of cute."

43

I'm happy to not think about Colleen. "I'll take a look at it. Which reminds me: do you know how to get something on YouTube? A guy at my school wants me to make him famous."

"Sure. What do you want to submit?"

"A piece of *High School Confidential,* maybe."

"It's no big deal, really. You just, like, log in, hit the Upload Videos link, choose the right file, give your piece a title, then select the category. It sounds more complicated than it is. Why don't I come by and show you? I take the Gold Line to Sierra Madre all the time. You live in South Pasadena, right? I could bring my laptop, get off at Mission on the way, and meet you at Buster's for coffee or something, okay?"

"Absolutely."

"How about tomorrow?"

When we hang up, I fall backward onto my bed. A date. Okay, not a *date* date, but a coffee date. With somebody who's interested in the same things I'm interested in. I know I'm getting way ahead of myself. A.J.'s probably got a boyfriend just as cute as she is and with a functioning set of extremities. It'll still be fun. And maybe somebody from school will see me sitting with a mysterious girl, snap me on their cell, upload that to the Net, and I'll be on YouTube starring in *The Spaz Experiences a Shiver of Delight.* Maybe even Colleen will see it and eat her heart out.

I'm too excited to sleep, so I turn on the TV and check out Sundance and TCM. Too many earnest ecologists on the first one. But Turner Classics is showing—wouldn't you know it—*Sleepless in Seattle,* where Tom Hanks and Meg Ryan fall in love almost without ever meeting.

How does stuff like that happen, anyway? Not the Meg and Tom stuff, but the Ben and A.J. stuff. I'm thinking of meeting a girl and then there's a movie about meeting a girl.

I know—just a coincidence. Law of averages, with so many movies on TV and so many people watching. But it's still eerie. Like me meeting Colleen at the Rialto. What were the chances of that?

It makes me wonder if something (or Somebody) isn't in charge. But in the great scheme of things, if I was supposed to hook up with Colleen, we're talking about Somebody with a real sense of humor. A god from Comedy Central.

MEETING A.J. MAKES ME NERVOUS. I spend way too much time worrying about what to wear. Is there a pair of pants that will make this leg look straight? A shirt that'll put a nice triceps on that left arm? *That* arm. *That* leg. Not *my* or *mine.*

I decide on jeans and a long-sleeved polo shirt. I never wear anything but long sleeves. If there's a Hell and if I go there, I'll be the only person not in a tank top.

Treasure of the Sierra Madre is on. I turn the volume up so I can hear it while I'm in the bathroom, and I watch it in the mirror while I brush my teeth and especially when I'm right out of the shower, buck naked. I don't want to look down at that body if I don't have to.

So I concentrate on Bogart and Walter Huston and Robert Blake as the little boy who sells Bogart the winning lottery ticket.

What would I do without movies?

When I make it to the kitchen, Grandma's on the phone to another gazillionaire. But Grandma's an honest-to-God philanthropist and not just—as Colleen so delicately puts it—"another rich bitch." I eat an apple, then do some homework until it's almost time to meet A.J.

I walk as only I can up to Buster's. Past Vidéothèque, past the yoga studio, and past the big new bakery with a few tables outside. A couple of little kids are sitting with their mom. They're trying to get honey on chunks of fresh bread, and you can almost hear her thinking, *I wish I had a picture of this.*

They stop what they're doing, though, when they see me. I don't mind it when kids stare. They don't know C.P. They don't really get it. They think I'm interesting, and I hate it when their folks make them stop and the kids are, like, "Why?" and the mom has this sick, apologetic smile.

Colleen was like those kids. She thought my body was interesting. She was curious about it. Once when Marcie drove up to Santa Barbara to see a boyfriend, Colleen and I were at her house so I could use her camera and computer to work on *High School Confidential.* We ended up in the bedroom. And, among other things, Colleen picked up my almost useless, semiwithered arm and kissed it. That just killed me. Man, if she liked me enough to do that, why doesn't she call me back?

I get to Buster's and I'm faced with a dilemma — do I wait for A.J. on the platform or sit here until she gets off the Gold Line, at which point I'll wave jauntily?

She knows I'm a spaz, or at least I think she does. And if she's forgotten, then it's probably a good idea to just get that part over with fast.

So I wait at the light with three tweens, all of them checking their phones, texting and tweeting and saying *like* about twelve times per sentence. Weird way to hang out, though: talking to three other people.

I'm invisible to them. But then maybe everybody is except the cutest boy in school, the one who lights matches and lets them burn all the way down to his fingertips.

Then the train pulls up, half a dozen people get off, and one of them is A.J. She's wearing kneesocks, a plaid skirt, and a little beret thing pinned to her hair that matches her skirt. I can just hear Colleen: "Everything but a f**king bagpipe."

She's got a big smile, and her teeth are amazing. Movie-star teeth. Out comes her hand, and I shake it. She holds on while she says, "Just to make sure it's you, name a movie where a train station figures prominently."

"Three-ten to Yuma."

"Nice. How've you been, Ben?" She frowns. "'Been, Ben.' That sounded redundant."

"I'm okay. How about you?"

"Busy." She points across the street. "Let's score a table, okay?"

We cross in a little crowd of people, ten or so, and they're all faster than I am. I can see A.J. checking both ways for enraged motorists, and when we're almost at the curb, she touches my elbow. Just barely, just a nudge, but it makes me feel officially handicapped. She's the Girl Scout, and I'm the good deed for the day.

We find a table with some shade, and she puts her laptop down. "This is my treat," she says. "Name your poison."

"I can get it, okay?"

She doesn't look away. "I know you can, Ben. But I want to."

While she's gone, I tell myself, *Settle down,* Benjamin. *Don't blow this.*

I struggle to my feet so that when she comes back with the coffee, peppermint tea, and a bagel, I can help her.

Once we get situated, she butters her bagel and offers me half, which I say no thanks to.

"Brief Encounter," I blurt. "Another train station movie."

"And *Doctor Zhivago*. Lots of trains in that one." She chews vigorously and then asks, "Did you see my friend's video on YouTube?"

"Not yet."

She brushes invisible crumbs off her hands and opens her laptop. She hits a few keys, then just hands the whole thing to me. "Check it out."

It's called *Dog Bytes Dog,* and it's just this Rottweiler with a controller that he doesn't really use, but the quick cuts back and forth from the pooch to the *Reservoir Dogs* game make that not matter.

When I hand the Mac back over, she says, "It's getting tons of hits. If Rane had just sent in Bowser watching TV, no way. And even if it was Bowser watching *Reservoir Dogs* maybe, maybe not. I think the title was the clincher. I guess what I'm saying is, whatever you're going to submit has to be pretty sharp to get any kind of play. Anybody can upload anything. It's fine to just be funny or cute, but it's better if what you upload matters, right?"

"Absolutely."

She starts to pick up her plastic chair. "Let me scoot

over there and show you how to submit——" She stops in midsentence. "No, wait. You come to me. Because you are totally able, am I right?"

That smile of hers is pretty irresistible. So maybe that little touch on the elbow at the curb was a one-time thing. Nerves. "Maybe not totally able, but I can make it if I try."

So we sit side by side; she hits keys and points, and I take some notes. YouTube looks absolutely doable.

I say, "*High School Confidential* isn't digital. How do I get that done?"

"It's just a swap. I don't have the equipment, but I know somebody who does."

"Are you going to send in a clip from *Roach Coach*? Or have you already?"

She falls back in her chair dramatically. "Oh, God. You don't know about that? No, how could you? Oh, man. Five of those food-service guys I interviewed got deported because of my movie."

"No way."

"Oh, yeah. My friends are passing *Roach Coach* around, or parts of it, anyway. Just one computer to another. But somebody somewhere looks at that footage a whole other way. It's not, 'Boy, these are hardworking, interesting guys.' It's, 'Who's got a green card?'"

"And there's nothing you can do?"

She shakes her head. "I talked to my dad—he's a lawyer—and nada."

"Maybe filmmakers are like doctors: 'First do no harm.'"

She nods. "Sometimes I'm watching a documentary and the person it's about is sick or bleeding, and I think, *Hey, you with the camera! Put that down and do something!*" Then she takes a deep breath, runs both hands through her hair, and says, "Well, before we both give up our budding careers, tell me your all-time top-of-the-list number-one totally adored favorite movie."

"Just one?"

"Just one."

I think for a few seconds. "*Ghost World,* maybe."

"Oh, my God. Talk about alienated youth. Scarlett Johansson was so good in that."

I tilt my cup in her direction. "Your turn."

She looks down at the initials of people like B.K. and L.M., who loved each other so much, one of them carved up a table. "I'm embarrassed. Don't tell anybody, okay?"

"Don't worry."

"It's *The Searchers.*"

"Sure. John Wayne, Jeffrey Hunter, Natalie Wood."

"I think about John Wayne looking for Natalie Wood for five years, and I just want to cry."

Then she blushes. I try to remember if I've ever seen

Colleen blush. Colleen. Man, I think about her all the time. I don't want to, but I can't help it.

I tell A.J., "If I went missing, Grandma would just call up the chief of police. She knows everybody."

"That was her at the gallery, right? Really elegant lady. There's everybody else all in black looking like they're trying to absorb as much radiation as possible, and there she is in pastel cashmere separates."

"She pretty much totally took care of me after my dad died. Got killed, actually."

"What about your mom?"

I waggle one hand—the good one—in that back-and-forth, who-really-knows-I'm-not-sure-I-want-to-talk-about-it way. "Just out of the picture."

Then we watch the traffic for a while. Bicyclists pull up in those Cirque du Soleil spandex outfits. A dog on a leash angles toward A.J., who pets him.

Finally she says, "Well, look at us get all serious." She glances at her iPhone. "I should go. You know the You-Tube drill, right?"

"I think so, yeah."

"And we're gonna e-mail, okay? Talk on the phone. You go to the movies at the Rialto, right?"

"All the time."

"We could do that. Everybody I know loves the Rialto."

She's on her feet then, one hand out. I struggle a little but not too much. She holds on to my hand. "*Ghost World.* Good for you." Then a quick little kiss on the cheek like she probably does to everybody, and she's gone.

I sit down again. The first thing I think is — *nice.* She seems really nice. I'll e-mail her. I'll talk to her on the phone. I'll go to the Rialto with her and her friends, but I'll sit by her. I can't depend on Colleen. I never could.

After dinner I doze off watching Robert Mitchum in *The Friends of Eddie Coyle,* so when the phone rings, I paw for the receiver like a cop who already knows there's another body down by the river. I don't even get to say hello before I hear, "Where's Granny?"

I sit up straight. "Colleen?"

"Is she home?"

"She's at a fund-raiser."

"Start taking your clothes off."

"Where've you been, anyway? Why didn't you call me?"

"You don't get to ask those questions. All you get to do is kiss me all over. Deal or no deal?"

"I'm already in my pajamas."

"All buttoned up, too, I'll bet. Well, you do your one-handed best with those buttons, Quasimodo, and I'll get the rest. Now shut up and get to work. We're wasting time."

Thirty minutes later, Colleen is sprawled beside me. One hand, her left, mouses around—playing with my hair, pinching me, tickling. The sheets are tangled and damp. And I can't help but think, *Tangled sheets. Wow. I've seen that in a hundred movies!*

The blinds are half open, and the moonlight looks extra-fragile.

"I wish we could sleep," Colleen says. "I'm so sleepy."

I glance at the clock, then get out of bed and pick up my new camera. "You can sleep for twenty minutes if I can shoot some film."

She starts to roll over. "Want to see my tits?"

"No. It's not about that. It's about how you look in this light. Stay like you are."

"Wake me up before Grandma gets home."

"Don't worry."

I pull the covers up a little. I want part of the Firebird tattoo that erupts from her underpants, but I don't want the waistband. And I like the way one foot sticks out from under the sheet.

I adjust the blinds, then shoot another minute or two of film. It's easy to make her pretty because she is. Or could be. And I'm not sure *pretty* is the right word, anyway.

Finally I open the blinds as wide as they'll go and tilt the lamp on my desk. The oldest tats bleed and fade. There's a callus on her other foot. A bruise on her left shoulder, right beside the Grim Reaper tattoo — a skull smoking a cigar, a banner under that with the name Johnny Too Bad.

Then I sit at the desk, and play it all back on my Mac. Maybe my next movie is about her. She's what's on my mind. So I go over and wake up the most unlikely muse ever.

"Time to go home. Grandma will be back pretty soon."

She looks at me, tries to focus. "You're cute."

"You're half asleep." I tug at her. "C'mon."

She holds on tight. "I know I'm a pain in the ass sometimes, but don't give up on me. I'll be a better girlfriend. I promise."

Colleen picks me up for school every morning. We do homework together. I make sure she eats things that are at least slightly good for her. Grandma tolerates her.

Then one Friday, Oliver Atkins meets us in the parking lot. When I get out of her VW, he screams, "Well, if it isn't my Judy."

Colleen warns him, "Take it easy, Oliver. Ben is mine. All one hundred and twenty handicapped pounds of him."

"Fifty thousand hits so far," Oliver says, "and the beginning of I don't know how many meaningful dialogues."

I tell him, "You're welcome."

"You should thank me, Benjamin. I am going to put you on the map."

Colleen watches him prance away. "Did Oliver put the moves on you?"

I just look at her. "Get serious."

"Did you ask him why he wears that ridiculous hat with the feather on it? He looks like one of Robin Hood's extremely merry men from RumpRanger Forest."

"Don't take this the wrong way, but you're wearing panty hose that you've ripped up on purpose, shorts with holes in them, and a tank top with green zombie hands on your boobs. The phrase 'You should talk' occurs to me."

She drapes one arm around my shoulders. "Yeah, but I look hot; Oliver just looks gay."

"You don't know him like I do."

"What's that supposed to mean?"

"For *High School Confidential* I talked to Oliver for a long time. I told you what it's like making a documentary: you shoot an hour of film and use a minute and a half. So I know him."

"Are you saying he's not gay?"

"I'm saying he's not just gay."

We're on our way to class when she tells me, "I got a postcard from Ed. Boot camp is killing him."

"At least he's clean and sober."

"Get serious. He says he could get high every night if he wanted to."

I want to ask if she still likes him, but I don't want to hear the answer. I'm afraid he'll come back on leave bigger and stronger and better-looking than ever.

Instead I say, "I'll see you at lunch."

She grabs my T-shirt and pulls me in to her. "He's history, okay? He's poison. I can't be around him or guys like him ever."

I let one hand slip into the back pocket of her thrashed shorts. "I didn't say anything."

"I can read you like a book, Benjamin."

"Since I've seen you read, that doesn't exactly scare me."

Colleen pretends to beat on me and I pretend to cringe. I've seen kids do this a hundred times. Couples horsing around. Just regular kids. I like it that that's what Colleen and I are.

At noon, I beat her to the cafeteria, and I've barely settled down behind a chef's salad when my phone rings. It's A.J. She's in a hurry but wants to invite me and "anybody else" I want to bring to her house Saturday night. Just a few people. No big deal. Kind of a movie party.

Debra, one of the girls with babies who was in *High School Confidential,* sits down across from me and scowls till I hang up. When I do, she barks, "I don't want to be on YouTube."

"Fine. Don't be."

"It's all Oliver can talk about, but I don't want no

part of it. I'm sorry I said what I said about Molly being lighter-skinned and all. I mean, she is, but we talked about that and her little boy and my little girl, and now we help each other out sometimes with babysitting and shit, and I don't want hard feelings."

"Debra, I did the Oliver piece as a favor to him, okay? And kind of to just see if I could do it. I'm not going to use your part. Relax."

She stands up and tugs at her Los Angeles Lakers T-shirt. "You promise?"

"Absolutely."

Colleen steps right up beside her and gives her a little hip check. "Is everybody hitting on my boyfriend today?"

"He don't keep his promise," says Debra, "he'll see some real-life hitting." Then she flounces away.

Colleen sits down and takes a big bite out of a giant slice of pizza before she says, "What's the name of that movie where some kid journalist goes on tour with a rock band? It was on last night."

"*Almost Famous.* Billy Crudup, Kate Hudson, and Anna Paquin as Polexia Aphrodisia. It was about a real guy, a journalist named Cameron Crowe."

Colleen just shakes her head. "How do you remember all that? I can't remember what I read twenty minutes ago."

"I don't know. I just do."

"You don't even try?"

"I try to remember when I study for history or something. But with movies, they just kind of seep into me."

"Well, I wish math would seep into me."

We concentrate on the trays in front of us for a minute. Somebody drops a plate, and the whole cafeteria applauds. Colleen's a little twitchy all of a sudden. I reach for her hand, and she lets me hold it.

"Do you want to go to a party Saturday night at A.J.'s house?"

"Who's A.J.?"

"Just this girl I met. She's into movies, too."

"Since when are you meeting girls?"

"Since that night in Hollywood. At the gallery. You were busy with Nick, remember?"

"Oh, yeah. That loser."

"A.J. says it's Vampire Night. So we'll eat and watch a Bela Lugosi movie, probably."

Colleen pretends to ponder. "Let me see: would I rather go to a club and get high or watch a DVD about bloodsuckers with a bunch of eleventh-graders? What a dilemma!"

"Eight o'clock, all right? Or come at seven and eat with Grandma and me."

She shakes her head. "Granny makes me want to jump out a window. I'll pick you up at eight."

I WAIT BY THE DOOR LIKE FIDO, and when Colleen tools up, I make my way to the curb. It takes a little while, and I can see her drumming with both hands on the steering wheel.

She opens the door for me, and I fall into the seat, a move I've perfected.

"What's the address?" she asks.

"Linden Lane."

"I hate this girl already. Fucking Linden Lane. I live on Fourth Street. Why am I on dead-assed Fourth Street and she's on glamorous Linden Lane?"

I point across the street. A yellow SUV is parked in the driveway. "Marcie's back."

Colleen roars away from the curb without even looking. "Where's she been?"

"Some kind of retreat. She does that sometimes."

"Why can't I go on a retreat? I want to go on a retreat to Linden Lane and meditate with my butt in a tub of butter."

Colleen rants a lot, and there's no point in ranting back, much less being reasonable. I put my sick little left hand on her leg, and she reaches down and pats it.

"I'm all right," she says.

"I didn't say you weren't."

"I know what you're thinking."

"I'm not thinking anything."

"Bullshit. You're always thinking, Benjamin. If you really loved me, you'd stop that nasty habit."

We go north on Fair Oaks, then cut across Glenarm. The houses get nicer and nicer. Bigger and bigger lawns. When we're just a few blocks away from 6799, there's a little park: big, sandy area with swings and a slide. Benches made out of wrought iron and wood under cool, old-fashioned lights. Sitting on the one closest to us is a mom with her little girl. They're holding a book with big pages. Mom's got her arm around the kid who points, then looks up to see if she got it right.

"I don't get that," Colleen says. "I don't have the gene. Last thing in the world I want to do is sit in the middle of nowhere and say, 'No, that's not a kitty. It's a camel. But that's all right. Your daddy and I just love you to pieces!' I'd rather shoot myself."

"If these were the first few frames of a Sam Raimi film, pretty soon something unspeakably evil would come out of that gardener's shed."

"If that's going to happen, I can skip A.J.'s party and stay here and cheer."

Instead Mom lifts her daughter up and cuddles her, so Colleen steps on the gas.

A.J.'s house turns out to be pretty impressive. Not a mansion, thank God, or Colleen would never shut up. There's a wide, curving driveway, a mega-green lawn, a couple of urns beside the steps leading up to the porch. Not Keats urns, with maidens and fauns and gods. These are artier, covered with little tiles and littler fragments of mirror. But not cheesy. Somebody took a lot of time with those. And then put a fat price tag on the side.

We walk past three cars lined up behind each other: a Subaru Outback that needs to go through a car wash, a Volvo a couple of years old, and a '65 Mustang convertible. White and in perfect condition. I could see A.J. in that car, either behind the wheel or sitting beside the cooler-than-me driver.

When we get to the door, I take a look at us. Thanks to Grandma, most of my clothes are preppy — khakis and oxford-cloth shirts. Normal clothes. Part of my disguise. Tonight, Colleen's in a supershort dress and really high heels. A lot of skin showing and a lot of tattoos on that skin.

I lift the huge brass horseshoe and tap a couple of times. She says, "My doorbell doesn't work. People just shout through the flimsy plywood."

"What if I buy you a big knocker for your birthday?"

"Then I'd have three. Two little ones and a big one. Whatever happened to symmetry?"

Just then, A.J. opens the door and flashes that arc-light smile.

"Good evening," says Colleen, "my crippled friend and I have come a long way to talk to you about Jesus."

A.J. puts out one hand. "Amy Jane Moore. Agnostic."

That makes Colleen smile. She tells A.J. her name, then adds, "I like your house. I want to live here."

"I don't blame you. Come on in."

Inside it's mostly red and yellow. Huge windows looking out on a garden with green-and-white patio furniture. Blue vases with real sunflowers. Four kids sit by a coffee table as big as a Conestoga wagon wheel.

The guys turn out to be Rane (with an *a*) and Conrad. The girls — twins, no less — are Danielle and Denise.

Rane's in REI pants and heavy shoes with lug soles. Definitely the Subaru. The twins are slouchy — loose flannel shirts over floppy Ts, baggy jeans, Vans with no socks. Not the same but very similar. Ash-colored hair cut to look like lazy mullets, if there is such a thing. They drive the Volvo.

That leaves Conrad: lean and mean, spiky-looking hair, blond at the tips. Shorts that fit. A cut on his cheek. From lacrosse, probably. The Mustang for sure.

He and I are introduced and I get, "Yeah, hi."

He's already written me off. We're not going to shoot hoops or ski together. I'm not tight with the people he hangs with. I'm a nobody with a limp.

But none of them can take their eyes off Colleen. The twins breathe through their mouths. They have an at-the-zoo look: *So that's the rare snow leopard!* Rane probably imagines wrestling a bear while she cringes in the moss and her skirt rides up higher on her long, white legs.

One corner of Conrad's mouth twitches. His eyes close deliberately, then open slowly. He's the one Colleen's mother would pick out of the crowd: the apex predator.

"Want to show me where you hide the silver?" Colleen says to A.J.

A.J. asks, "Ben?"

"You guys go ahead. I'm okay." I really don't want to hobble around while A.J. points out the paintings of her ancestors.

"Get something to eat. We'll be right back."

I take a little plate and make my clumsy way around the table. Rane stands up to make things easier for me. Conrad is busy texting, so I slide past.

I take some black olives, a couple of stuffed grape leaves, some hummus, some pita chips. Then manage to sit down without anything bouncing off my plate.

"How do you and—" Danielle begins, and then Denise finishes, "—A.J. know each other?"

"Um, from a gallery show. She brought *Roach Coach*, and I brought something I called *High School Confidential*."

Rane says, "That's right. A.J. said you got, like, a minute of that on YouTube. Something about a gay guy from your school. Conrad got a ton of YouTube hits about six months ago."

I look his way. He's everything I want to be. Or wanted to be once. That wishing crap never got me anywhere. I ask politely, "What was it about?"

"I was on my way home from a party and saw these cops whaling away on this Hispanic guy they'd pulled over, so I shot it with my cell and sent it the next day."

"It was—" says Danielle.

Her sister finishes for her. "—very cool."

Danielle begins, "Very—" and Denise asserts, "—Rodney King."

Conrad asks me, "How many hits did you get?"

I take a bite of pita bread before I answer. "I'm not sure. Oliver kept track, though. Thousands, I guess."

Rane nods. "Sweet."

"And it's okay with you to promote that agenda?" Conrad asks.

"What agenda?"

Denise starts, "The gay—"

"—one," adds Danielle.

Just then A.J. and Colleen come back.

"You should make a documentary about this place," Colleen says. "Call it *Bucks Out the Butt*." She walks toward the satchel I'd hung on a hat rack in the foyer. "Did you show these guys your new camera?" She brandishes it. That's the right word, too. Pretty much everything Colleen does is a challenge. Meet her on the dueling grounds at dawn, in the street outside the dry-goods store at high noon. Just try and outshoot or outwit her.

Conrad reaches for it. And, wouldn't you know it, he treats it like it was his, like he's had one just like it but now has the newer model. Pushes the right button, then points it at Colleen, who says, "You're never going to get in my pants, pretty boy. You're way too predictable."

He blushes, and a muscle in his jaw twitches. The twins gawk. He tosses the camera to me, and I make a lucky catch.

"May I see that?" Rane asks.

I hand it over.

"Let's eat," says A.J., "and then we'll watch the movie."

Conrad heads somewhere, the library, probably, to borrow a heavy candlestick from Colonel Mustard. Danielle and Denise start to chatter about getting into college. Danielle looks at me and starts a question: "How many community service hours—"

"—do you have?" Denise finishes.

I shake my head. "None."

"Oh, you need as many as you—"

"—can get. Don't you, Rane?"

He holds the camera up, and I can tell he's used one before. He shoots while he answers, "It looks good on your college apps."

The twins flank Colleen, who's piling food on her plate. "How about —"

"— you?"

Colleen pauses, "How about me what?" She's taller than they are, and she looks like somebody from another part of the continent. Or world. Or galaxy.

"How many hours —"

"— of community service do you have?"

Colleen pretends to think the question over. "Well, I went to a nursing home and gave a bunch of old guys hand jobs once — does that count?"

Rane catches it on film, getting the twins' expressions, then Colleen's smirk. When she reaches for a deviled egg, he zooms in on the droopy neckline of her dress, hoping for a peek at her breasts. The only ones I've ever seen up close and personal. And maybe the only ones I'll ever see.

Should I be mad that Rane's scamming on her, and with my camera to boot? I don't think so. Colleen can take care of herself. And I don't blame him for looking at her. I do it all the time.

Conrad comes back, waits until the twins make room for him, then sits between them and starts to text again.

A.J. points to a pile of DVDs. "Somebody pick one." Then she asks me to help her with something in the kitchen. My pulse goes up a notch or two: that move is in every French farce—meeting in the kitchen, making out in the pantry, a maid in a little skirt with eyes for the husband.

More tile in there, a wicker basket of oranges. A whole basketful. Nobody could eat that many oranges. Brass pots and pans hanging on a wrought-iron rack over the stove. An open window with a breeze. Yellow light pours in, a yellow somewhere between tawny and cream. I want to look out the window and make sure there isn't a cinematographer in the gazebo, or some guy with a dimmer board dialing in the perfection.

A.J. arranges some tall blue glasses on a tray. "Where did you find her?"

She sounds totally curious, but not mean.

I tell her, "Colleen goes to my school. And we just kind of ran into each other at the movies one night."

She moves the glasses around. "Why is she so snarky?"

I shrug. "Ask her."

"She ticked Conrad off."

"She read his mind."

She starts to cut up a melon, really taking her time about it. "Conrad's okay."

"If you say so."

"I'm serious. That *Black and Tan* video he shot was really good."

"Is that what he called it? The Black and Tans were Brits who beat up on the Irish."

"Right, but he meant to evoke Rodney King and the Hispanic guy."

"And everybody who watches YouTube knew that?"

"Obviously some of them did."

We stand there. I barely know her, and we're arguing over Conrad. Does she stand up for all her friends, or is Conrad somebody special? Finally I tell her, "You'd better carry those glasses; I've been known to spill things. I'll hold the door."

She puts a hand on my good arm. "I'm glad you came. Colleen, too. It's just . . . It's hard to explain. I've known Conrad forever."

"Sure."

"I've known all those guys. Rane and I learned to ski together. The twins and I were in preschool. They're really, really smart. They've already got early admission to Yale."

Out in the other room, Colleen's sitting by Rane, and Conrad's between the twins. They're talking about vampires.

Denise says, "If a vampire comes across a sack of rice—"

Danielle adds, "—he has to count every grain. And if you want to find a vampire's grave—"

Denise steps in, "—you need a virgin boy on a virgin horse. You lead them—"

Back to Danielle, "—through the cemetery, and the horse will stop at the vampire's grave."

Colleen says, "Oh, so the horse has to be a virgin. No wonder I couldn't find that pesky grave," and everybody laughs except Conrad, who looks up from his iPhone to tell us, "Vampire movies are political. It's always one class feeding on another. Doesn't matter if it's F. W. Monroe or Catherine Hardwicke."

The twins nod and file that information away, probably for their first essay at Yale.

"It's not Monroe," I say. "It's Murnau. F. W. Murnau. When he made *Nosferatu,* he pretty much used the Bram Stoker novel as the script. Mrs. Stoker ended up suing him."

Conrad says, "I beg your pardon?"

"I said he almost plagiarized —"

"Not that. The director."

"Oh, that. His name isn't Monroe."

Conrad scoots forward on the brown leather couch. "I'm pretty sure it is."

Colleen sets her plate on the big coffee table. She digs in her purse and throws a twenty beside the grape leaves. She looks at Conrad. "Want to put your money where your pretty mouth is?"

He just shakes his head at her effrontery, but he comes up with the money and tosses it, wadded up like a Kleenex, beside Colleen's, which is not only smoothed out but creased down the middle. I wonder if somebody tucked that into her mother's thong last night. And did she give it to Colleen, or did Colleen just take it?

A.J. looks up from her phone, where she's asked the omniscient Google for the answer. "It's Murnau, Conrad."

"Well, crap!"

Rane, outdoorsman and peacemaker, suggests, "Let's just watch Bela Lugosi."

Colleen shakes her head. "I know that movie," she says. "He's tall, dark, and thirsty, and she's a stupid twit who sleeps with her window open in Transylvania. Let's gamble some more." She looks at Conrad. "You against Ben, honey buns. Twenty bucks a pop, and your idolaters here will make up the questions, which have to be about tonight's topic — vampires."

Idolaters. Underneath the tats and the attitude is a really smart girl. If I'm a tree that's been hit by lightning, Colleen is a tree that grew the wrong way. Buffeted by high winds, maybe. Relentless high winds.

The twins are positively quaking with excitement. They look at A.J., who shrugs and says, "Okay, I guess."

Colleen winks at me and licks her lips. I'm nervous but totally up for this. In a fight, it'd be easy for Conrad to knock me down. Or literally run circles around me, if we had to race. He's probably smarter than me about everything else in the world except movies. Nobody knows more about movies than I do. This is the fight at the O.K. Corral, as far as I'm concerned.

A.J. goes to one of the drawers in a big, antiquey-looking desk and comes back with yellow pads and thick black pens.

She says, "The rest of us will make up questions using Wikipedia or Screen Rant. You two write your answers down and hold them up when we say to."

Conrad points at Colleen. "No input from her. I don't trust her."

"I'm just the banker," she says.

The twins come up with the first question.

"From *The Lost Boys*—" says Denise.

And Danielle finishes, "—name any four principal actors."

I watch Conrad write fast and then hesitate. It doesn't take me long. Then we wait.

Colleen taunts him. "Any time in this century."

I eat another stuffed grape leaf. Conrad's money still looks like a cud. It doesn't mean anything to him. There's always more where that came from.

"Time's up," says A.J.

Conrad pouts. "I've got three!"

Colleen reminds him, "But to win you had to name four." She looks at me. "Who are they, Ben?"

"Jason Patric, Corey Feldman, Corey Haim, and

Kiefer Sutherland. Among others like Jami Gertz and Dianne Wiest."

Colleen grabs for the cash. "Next?"

The others huddle, then A.J. asks, "In *Nosferatu,* what was the vampire's name, and who played him?"

Conrad and I write fast.

When A.J. asks, "Ready?" we both nod and show our answers: Count Orlok, played by Max Schreck.

"Tie," says Colleen, tossing out another bill. "Double or nothing."

More huddling. A.J. taps her iPhone a couple of times. Then she asks, "In *Shadow of the Vampire,* who played Max Schreck?"

I can see Conrad's pen poised over the lined notebook, and I know he doesn't know. *Shadow of the Vampire* is a cool movie where the guy playing the vampire might really be a vampire.

Colleen sinks into the couch and puts both arms along the back of it. Ed, her old boyfriend, used to sit like that, daring anybody to get even an inch into his space.

Sometimes she stumbled around after Ed like one of Dracula's pale brides, and he fed off her, in a way. In vampire lore it's not necessarily blood they're after. It's life essence. And she's got gallons of that.

"Time," says A.J.

I hold up my notebook and say, "Willem Dafoe."

Conrad rips a blank sheet of paper out of his note-book and hurls it toward the windows.

Colleen tosses out another twenty. "Tell me when you've had enough."

"Bite me," Conrad snarls.

"You wish."

I wear him down. He doesn't even know *Near Dark*, a terrific Kathryn Bigelow film, but we tie with *Love at First Bite*. I get the question about *Cronos*, and we tie again with *Horror of Dracula*, a Hammer film with Christopher Lee and the great Peter Cushing.

He doesn't remember that Josh Hartnett was in *30 Days of Night* and just freezes on *From Dusk Till Dawn*, the stupid Robert Rodriguez movie about a bar where the pole dancers are all vampires.

And then he's broke.

Colleen stands up and tells me, "C'mon, baby. We've done all the damage we can do here."

At "baby," A.J. does a classic double take. She'd clearly never thought of me as "baby" material before. Just a gimp with a limp who could still hold a camera.

I hold out my good hand to Conrad. "That was fun."

He keeps his powerful mitts to himself. "I'd know all that useless bullshit, too," he says, "if all I did was sit in my room all day."

I nod. "That's how I did it."

A.J. follows Colleen and me to the door. "Not quite

the evening I planned," she says, "but that isn't really a complaint." She looks at Colleen. "Nice meeting you. Really. I mean it."

"I know you do. I'm an interesting person with many fine qualities. C'mon, Ben."

I wish A.J. wouldn't watch me hobble all the way to the car, but she does, standing in the open door with the light behind her. I have to admit — she and Conrad make the perfect Abercrombie & Fitch couple.

Colleen starts the car, then lets it idle while she digs around in her purse and finds a joint. Which she immediately fires up. So I ask, "Is this your idea of clean and sober?"

"Lighten up," she says. "Old Conrad didn't know what hit him. You mopped the floor with his privileged ass." She reaches, pulls me to her, and kisses me hard. Her breath is thick and smoky. "That kind of stuff gets me hot."

We make out in front of A.J.'s house for a few minutes. I wish everybody would come out and see us. I don't want them to think I'm just the handicapped kid and Colleen's my sexy attendant.

But pretty soon, she puts the car in gear and we speed away.

"You like A.J., don't you?" she asks.

"She's nice. The last time anybody asked me to a party, I was five years old and I had to wear a pointy hat."

She says, "Guys like you don't go to her private school. You know that, right?"

"Gimps don't?"

"That's right. Gimps don't. She's curious about you. But that doesn't make you gimpalicious. That doesn't mean you're boyfriend material."

I like dueling with Colleen. Compared to her, Conrad was a walk in the park. I tell her, "I thought I was *your* boyfriend."

"That's right. And don't you forget it."

Colleen hangs a hard right and glides to a stop. The houses all around us are big and mostly dark. Only a light on here and there. Maybe a maiden with her window open, reading by candlelight, half afraid she'll hear the rustle of wings and look up and there he'll be.

Colleen turns the engine off, lights another joint, leans against the door. Sprawls, actually. There are buttons on the front of her dress, and she undoes two of them. She tugs, then peers down. "Oh, my God. Forgetful old me. No bra."

I take out my camera and tell her, "Don't move, okay? Don't do anything else. You're perfect."

"Give me your hand," she says. "The sick one. He never gets any action."

I love the way the smoke looks pouring out of her nostrils, curling and making letters in the air I can almost recognize. She's got one arm up over her head, the joint between two fingers.

"C'mon, baby. What are you waiting for?"

I can do it—get those maimed and innocent fingers over to her. And I can hold the camera, too. And it watches her lead that hand between the buttons and into her dress.

"Can you feel that, Benjamin?"

I nod, too dry-mouthed to really talk. But I manage to croak, "Yes."

She widens her eyes and delivers the next sentence like a mad scientist: "It's alive. Alive, I tell you!" Then she laughs and pulls me toward her. Almost onto her, plenty close enough for her to get her hand in my hair and start kissing me.

And that's what we're doing when a car pulls up behind us and a whirling red light makes the whole scene look like a bloodbath.

THIRTY MINUTES LATER, we're sitting on a bench in the police station while the cops who brought us in joke around with each other and do paperwork. I've got my head in my hands. Colleen just takes everything in.

"This place is a gold mine, Ben. I'll go over and stand by the Wanted posters, and you take my picture."

I hiss at her, "You were smoking dope."

She shakes her head. "When they lit us up, I flicked that roach so far, it's probably in Santa Monica. What are you thinking — that they'd find my DNA on it? No fucking way. They smelled a little ganja, and now they're trying to scare us straight. All they're really doing is calling your grandma."

"And your mom."

"That could take a while. She hasn't exactly got her cell phone in her thong."

One of the cops comes over. He's big, and the gear on his utility belt must weigh thirty pounds. There's a pistol and a radio, pepper spray, a cell phone and a nightstick. He lets his left hand rest on the butt of his gun.

"Officer," Colleen says, "we want to confess. We're guilty of desire. But we want to pay our debt to society, then lead upright lives from now on. Maybe buy a little mom-and-pop store, live upstairs and give the beat cops free coffee."

Officer Armstrong — he's wearing a name tag — says to me, "Your girlfriend here's got quite a mouth on her."

"That's why he likes me, isn't it, Ben?"

The cop behind the desk says, "Ms. Minou. Step up here, please. We're having trouble getting hold of your mother."

Officer Armstrong sits down beside me. "I guess I know what you're doin' with her, and I can't say that I blame you. That dress of hers is something else — what there is of it. But she looks like trouble to me, son. You're a pretty clean-cut kid. She's the pothead."

I like the way he's talking to me, too. Man-to-man. Not man-to-spaz. He doesn't ask me how I manage to have a girlfriend like Colleen with only half of me in good working order.

Just then Grandma comes through the front door. She's in cashmere, as usual. Something dark to set off the pallor, because I've never seen her look so washed out.

Officer Armstrong goes right to her with his hand out. Grandma takes it and holds on. I hear him say, "He's fine."

"I knew I could count on you."

Oh, crap. So it wasn't man-to-man. They're in this together. She's got him in her pocket. He'll say whatever she wants him to say.

Grandma turns to the desk sergeant. "Is there anything you need me to sign?"

He shakes his head. "He's learned his lesson, Mrs. Bancroft. We won't be seeing him in here again."

She motions for me. "Benjamin, let's go home."

"C'mon, Colleen."

Grandma's voice could quick-freeze vegetables.

"That girl is not going anywhere with us, Benjamin. She's got a mother."

"We're just going to drop her off. Her mother's working."

Grandma takes hold of my wrist. "Come along, Benjamin. My patience is wearing thin."

I look at Colleen helplessly.

"Don't worry about me," she says icily. "I can take care of myself."

On Monday, I wait outside her English class, but she doesn't show. At noon, she's not in the cafeteria. I'm too nervous to eat, so I look in the Pit and by the candy machines. I ask a couple of stoners and then this skate punk who used to hang around with Ed. Nobody's seen her.

And then, right after French, there she is. Different clothes from Saturday night, so I know she's been home. She's carrying this ugly purse that's black-and-white and covered with some kind of coarse hair. It's made out of somebody's pony, I swear to God.

"Well," she says, getting right in my face, "if it isn't Mr. Chickenshit."

She swings that purse at me. I block with my good arm, lose my balance, and go down onto the polished linoleum.

"What'd I do?"

The hall goes dead quiet. Everybody watches.

"It's what you didn't do, Benjamin. It's three o'clock in the morning before the cops figure out my mom's never coming. I thought I was your girlfriend. Why didn't you stay with me?" Colleen hits me again, and I curl up. "Jesus Christ, Ben. I finally meet one guy I think I can trust just a little, and look what happens." She wields that hideous purse like an ax. One blow for every word. "Nobody plays me, Ben. Nobody." Then she starts to swing wildly. "Why don't you take a picture of this, you cold-hearted bastard?"

And she doesn't stop whaling away at me until some teacher comes storming out of his classroom, gets both arms around her waist, and literally carries her away, kicking and screaming.

Colleen gets suspended and sent to Alternative School. Dumbbell High. Bad Girl Academy. Vice-principals almost never punish the handicapped, but Grandma puts me in solitary. The Hole. Carpeted and air-conditioned, but I'm totally alone. She and I don't even eat together. I've never seen her so mad.

A week goes by. Not a word from Colleen. Grandma thaws out a milliliter at a time. We don't talk about what happened, but we do talk. A little, anyway.

On Friday, A.J. e-mails and wants to go to the Rialto, but I tell her there's no way. So she calls Grandma, says how her mom knows Grandma from some board or other. Says she needs to talk to me about this documentary she's thinking of making. Couldn't I get a pass for just one afternoon?

The next day I'm dressed and in the living room, waiting for A.J. like I used to wait for Colleen. Grandma glides up beside me. It's weird to see her mad like a regular parent. I was always such a good boy. And then I met You-Know-Who.

"Home by six o'clock, Benjamin, and not a minute after."

"Yes, ma'am."

"If anything happens, I want you to call me."

"Nothing will happen. We're just going to the movies, and then maybe Buster's. That's it. Thanks for letting me do this. Really."

She picks an invisible piece of lint off my shirt. This is her way of saying she's not totally steamed anymore. Grandma was never much of a toucher. When I was little, she would read to me, then tuck me in and almost kiss me good night. Half an inch away. A quarter. Three millimeters. Never all the way.

Colleen was a toucher. Colleen went all the way and a little past that.

Grandma says, "I just want you to know that I am still this far from taking your camera away." Her thumb and forefinger are half an inch apart.

"I understand. And I don't blame you. It won't happen again. Nothing like that will ever happen again."

I see Marcie across the street, down on her knees in front of a palm tree.

"Can I go over and say hi?" I ask. "A.J. can just pull into her driveway."

"I still want to meet this young woman."

"Sure. Absolutely."

Waiting at the curb, I look both ways like a good boy. Marcie sees me coming, stands up, and brushes at her pants.

"Did you have to dig your way out?" she asks.

"So you know what happened."

"Mrs. B. came over."

"I really screwed up."

She taps the trowel against the palm, then rubs at it. "Rite of passage. The road to adulthood goes directly through a police station, followed by a dark and dangerous forest."

"I just left Colleen sitting there in that stupid police station. She's never going to talk to me again."

"You don't know that."

"I do, too. She would've said so, but she was busy hitting me with her purse."

"I threw a Calphalon saucepan at my first husband and talked to him an hour later."

I take a step closer. "I had a girlfriend, Marcie. A

real girlfriend. She trusted me, and I let her down."

"You'll know better next time."

"She hates me. I'm never going to see her again."

"I meant with somebody else."

"Oh, yeah. Girls are lined up around the block. They just can't wait to take long limps on the beach with me."

Marcie glances up the street. "Mrs. B. said you were going out with some friends. Maybe you'll just do that for a while. Not everybody has a partner."

"You don't understand. I wouldn't have these friends without Colleen. She made me feel like I was just another guy, maybe with a few problems, but basically okay. If it wasn't for her, I couldn't even have talked to them. I'd have thought, *What do they want with me? I'm nobody.*"

"Colleen didn't help you make a movie, Ben. You did that on your own. And it was terrific. People loved it. They loved you."

"You helped me with *High School Confidential*. You told me I was special and talented and all that. But you're a grown-up. Grown-ups say stuff like that to kids." I pointed to my heart. "But Colleen made me feel it."

Marcie walks right up and puts her arms around me. Holds on for a couple of seconds. Pats me hard. Lets me go. Says softly, "Talk to me about your next movie."

I have to swallow hard before I can say, "It's called *The Adventures of Colleen the Cat*."

"Because she always lands on her feet, right? Nice title. How far along are you?"

"I don't know. Three or four scenes, maybe. But that's all there'll ever be."

"Want to show me?"

"My friends are supposed to be here."

"I don't see any friends. What are we waiting for?"

I get across the street and back in four minutes. Not bad for a spaz. We don't even go inside. Marcie just finds a shady spot in her yard. She holds my little camera and I watch over her shoulder.

She starts with Colleen in bed. My bed. Then that scene at the Norton Simon Museum when she melted down, the night at A.J.'s with Conrad and the other kids, and after that when we were parked.

Marcie sits back. "How did you get that part where you were making out? I mean, you've got one hand in her shirt, but you're still holding the camera."

"I've got two hands, or a hand and a half. Basically I wanted the shot."

"And she was okay with that?"

"You know Colleen. She's kind of an exhibitionist, anyway."

Marcie frowns. "My guess is that men have used Colleen all her life. Now you're using her, too."

"I was making a movie about her. I can't do that if she isn't in it. It's not like I'm forcing her to do anything."

"And you think she knows what's really in her best interest?"

I point at the camera. "There's good stuff in there. That scene with her at A.J.'s party is terrific, and the part where she's half asleep in my bedroom and the light is coming in. She's sexy and gorgeous. It's not like I'm making her look ugly."

Marcie nods. "Those are well done. I agree."

"But you think I shouldn't be doing it."

Marcie rubs her face with both hands. "I wonder sometimes what Colleen would be like if somebody just loved her and didn't want anything from her."

Just then, a red Honda CR-V pulls up in front of the house.

"Go on," Marcie says. "Have a good time. We can talk about this later if you want."

A.J. and Rane get out and wave. I can see Grandma peering through the blinds and maybe even nodding a little: this is not a date with a tattooed stoner but with sun-tanned young people who floss regularly.

Except that Colleen and I didn't really date. She drove me places, and we did things that scared me and made me glad to be alive.

I lead the way down the sidewalk, open the door, and in we go. I do the honors. Rane shakes Grandma's hand.

A.J. says, "I'm really happy to meet you, Mrs. Bancroft. My mom thinks so highly of you."

I look for the teleprompter. Did she actually say that?

Rane throws one arm across my shoulders like we're chums at camp. "And I promise we'll keep our eyes on this bad boy."

Grandma frowns. "This is not a laughing matter, young man."

A.J. says, "When I got picked up, my mom was just as upset as you were. In a way it was a real learning experience, and what I learned was, I never want that to happen again as long as I live."

"I can only hope," Grandma says, "that Ben learned that same lesson."

She shakes A.J.'s hand again, then Rane's. She smooths the collar of my hand-pressed shirt. Not her hands, of course. Or mine. Rane, A.J., and I make our way to the car.

"Thanks, you guys," I say when I'm sure the door is closed and Grandma can't hear.

"Well," A.J. says, "it was either bullshit your grandma or send over a cake with a file."

I look at her. "You mean the cops never picked you up?"

"Are you kidding? My mom'd kill me." She digs in her purse for keys. "I know it's not very far, but let's drive. These shoes are cute, but they're not real practical."

Her shoes are plenty practical. She's just coddling the handicapped. Colleen hated to walk anywhere, but she was usually wearing totally impractical four-inch heels, so her already killer legs could stop traffic. And if we did walk from the car to some club, she'd outpace me, then taunt me: "C'mon. What are you, crippled?" Then she'd saunter back and kiss me so hard, my teeth hurt.

A.J. opens the back door for me. Holds it open. Hovers slightly. What does she think I'm going to do, fall down?

But her Honda is way different from Colleen's beater. That, I fell into; this I have to climb toward. So I struggle a little. A.J. starts to reach for the seat belt and buckle me in like I'm a sack of flour or Stephen Hawking, but I give her a look and she backs off.

Rane asks, "So were you and Colleen really smoking a joint when the cops showed up?"

"How do you know about that?"

"It's the electronic age," he says, holding up his phone. "Everybody knows everything."

"She was smoking. But she threw it away before they got to the car. I don't know why they took us in. Basically we were just sitting there, talking about the party." What I was also doing with my camera and my hands is none of their business.

A.J. says, "The twins are still talking about that night. How did you remember all that movie lore, anyway? That was very cool."

"Conrad didn't think so."

"He doesn't lose at anything very often. And, anyway, he was in a snit from arguing with his father."

"All he does," says Rane, "is argue with his father."

I tell them, "Well, as far as remembering stuff goes, Conrad was right. All I used to do was sit in my room and watch Turner Classics or DVDs from the video store or go to the Rialto. That was pretty much my so-called life."

We get lucky and park almost under the marquee. A.J. and Rane wave away my offer to buy the tickets, so we all pay for ourselves because this is a field trip.

A.J. shakes her head when I ask her if she wants any snacks. Rane pats one of his many pockets and whispers, "I've got gorp."

I know everybody who works in the Rialto, and when Sonia, who's scooping popcorn today, asks where I've been, I tell her, "Jail."

She laughs and the piercings in her eyebrows glitter. She can't picture me in trouble. I'm Ben the crippled moviegoer, Ben the loser in the dark.

Inside, Rane asks right up front, "Want to sit on the aisle, Ben? Probably easier for you, right?"

"A little, yeah."

So he files in, then A.J., then me. I met Colleen in the Rialto. Not five rows from here.

But *The Third Man* makes me forget that and

everything else. I love black-and-white, anyway, and the director and cinematographer order the light around. There are so many great scenes with Orson Welles and Joseph Cotten. Even their in-the-movie names are super-cool: Harry Lime and Holly Martins.

My favorite scene is a really quiet one. Holly is talking to Harry's old girlfriend Anna. Everybody thinks Harry is dead. Holly even went to the funeral. When Anna's cat snubs Holly and escapes out the window, she says that the cat didn't like anybody but Harry. And a minute later there's a mysterious man in an alley, and the cat is curled up at his feet!

Every now and then, Rane whispers to A.J. or she leans toward me and says, "I love this part."

I fall into the movie like I always do. I'm in postwar Vienna. I buy and sell on the black market. I'm Holly in love with Anna and I'm Harry on the run in the sewers of Vienna.

The lights go up. "Wow," says Rane. "I've seen that about five times, and I could see it again right now."

A.J. leads us out. Her blue pants are tight, and her butt is way cute. Rane's checking her out, too.

He whispers, "When we go hiking, I always let her take point."

I blush, but thanks to the dim lighting in the Rialto, he doesn't notice. What a dumb thing to do. I know how guys talk.

"Want to go to Buster's?" A.J. asks. "Get coffee or something?"

We drive over and on the way talk about *The Third Man*. Rane says it'd be fun to go to Vienna and find all the places that were in the movie, like the cemetery where Harry was buried (though he really wasn't), the theater where Anna worked, that kiosk with the secret door that led down into the sewers.

The first thing I think is this: *He could actually do that.* He and A.J. and the twins and Conrad. They could ask their parents and use their Visa cards and get on a plane to Europe.

At Buster's we score a table outside, and Rane says it's his treat. A.J. waits to see if I'm going to topple over after I drop into my chair, then she sits down, too.

I ask her, "Have you been to Europe?"

"Oh, yeah. You?"

"Grandma doesn't like airplanes."

"Do you?"

"I guess. I've never been on one."

"No way."

She sounds like I've just told her that I have a ferret in my back pocket.

"I used to see a lot of doctors and therapists and stuff, so I think Grandma kind of coddled me."

"You get around okay. You could totally fly if you wanted to. You'd even get to board early."

It's a stretch, because Grandma wouldn't want to. But who'd want her there, anyway? And if right after graduation I went with people she knew and liked and trusted, maybe . . . People like A.J.

Rane puts down his little cardboard tray and hands things around. "How'd the cat get down from the third floor?" he asks. "Holly's talking to Anna in her apartment on the third floor, okay? Then a minute later the cat is curled up at Harry's feet. How'd he get there?"

A.J. turns to me. "Rane is the blooper guy."

"Continuity guy, thank you. Like, in Anna's apartment the cat is black-and-white, but when she's down in that alley with Harry, it's a different cat. Not totally, but different. And you know that balloon-man sequence? First time we see him, he's got, like, twenty-five balloons. In the next shot, there're, like, twelve."

I suggest, "Maybe a blue-light special on balloons?"

A.J. says, "And the cat could've gone down the stairs. Cats are fast."

I like sitting and talking about movies. The only ones I'm not up on are really recent, and I missed those because I was out with Colleen. And I try not to think about how much fun that was compared to what I used to do, which was hide in the dark and watch other people live.

Rane looks at his watch and says, "I need a refill, and then I've gotta do some errands for my mom. You guys ready to go pretty soon?"

A.J. and I nod and watch him disappear.

"Do you want to do something with me?" she asks. "In a day or two, maybe? My dad knows about this jockey out at the racetrack who's, like, sixteen and just tearing things up. I'd like to interview him. Did you see that *Jockeys* show on Animal Planet?"

"Except for movies, I don't watch a lot of TV."

"It's kind of soap opera-ish. That cute girl from Canada and her boyfriend and all those horses falling down and stuff. I'll bet we could do better than that."

We?

I tell her, "Sure, I'll ride out there with you."

"Great." She grins at me. She grabs my good hand and shakes it, like we just made some kind of deal.

So. Maybe Marcie is right. Not everybody has a partner. They just have friends.

I get home from school and there's a message. Every time I see that blinking red light I hope it's Colleen, but it's not. It's A.J., and she wants to go out to Santa Anita Park early Saturday morning and get that jockey on film. Her dad can set the whole thing up: parking, backstretch passes, the whole nine yards. Am I up for that?

I wonder if Rane will be there. Then I wonder if I care. The three of us had fun at the Rialto and then Buster's. Just A.J. and me by ourselves would've been nerve-racking. What if we'd gone out for Italian food and ended up slurping the same strand of spaghetti, like those dogs in *Lady and the Tramp*?

It's stupid to think like that. I'm really not boyfriend material. And, anyway, I was Colleen's boyfriend, and look where that got me. In trouble, that's where. I'll settle for some friends with similar interests.

I'm thinking about punching in A.J.'s number when the doorbell rings. I tell Grandma I'll get it and head that way. I've got a funny feeling, anyway. We don't get door-to-door salesmen in South Pasadena, and it's not March, so I know it isn't the Girl Scouts selling cookies.

I open the door, and there stands Colleen, with what looks like everything she owns in a paper bag from the supermarket. She looks roughed up. Not by anybody so much as by life itself, I guess. Life with a capital *L*. Raccoon eyes, pale skin, dazed. If she told me she'd just woken up in a bathtub full of ice with one kidney missing, I'd have believed her. She opens her mouth, but nothing comes out.

"I guess I changed my mind," she says finally. "I love you after all."

"You're not carrying that dead pony purse, are you?"

"It's in the car."

"Okay, then you can come in."

She makes it through the door before she leans into me and takes a deep breath. She mutters into my shirt, "I don't know where else to go. Half my friends are stoners, and the other half don't like me."

I love the feel of her against me. "What happened?" I ask.

"My mom and I really got into it. She's fuckin' psycho. I slept in my car last night."

I point toward the living room. "Sit down, okay? I'll be right back."

Grandma is in the study when I knock.

"It's just for a couple of days," I tell her.

"Oh, Benjamin. Really."

"You're nice to people you don't even know. You send them money and medicine. All you have to do for Colleen is let her use the spare room." I move a little closer and sit in the same chair I sat in when I was little and she helped me with homework. I say, "That night at the police station, all we had to do was take her home. Five minutes out of our way. Instead we just left her there. That's why she was mad at me at school the next day, and I don't blame her."

Grandma sighs, like I knew she would. "No drugs."

I stand up. "Absolutely not. She knows that. Thanks a lot."

When I tell her everything's okay, Colleen gets a little color in her face, like her heart had been waiting to see what was going to happen.

I reach for that bag of clothes she's carrying, but she pulls it toward her. "They're dirty."

"I'll wash them for you."

She just stares at me. "You'd do that?"

"Sure. Just give me a bunch of quarters."

She elbows me, but not too hard. "Very funny."

I lead her down the long, carpeted hall. She's seen the room because she's been here when my grandmother was at yoga. She liked to romp around in her underpants and make me chase after her like Quasimodo and Esmeralda, so we've been pretty much everywhere in the house.

I open the door, and there it is — the queen-size bed, a purple-and-black kimono bedspread, stacked mahogany chests instead of plastic crates. Light, clear and sweet, pours in from the outside.

Colleen slumps against the door. "Fuck," she says, and starts to cry.

I tell her, "Go to bed. And give me those clothes."

She hands the bag over. "Do you want to kiss me or anything?"

"Do you want me to?"

"If you do."

Instead we just lean against each other like tired animals.

Then she says, "I should take a bath."

"Sure. Then try to sleep."

* * *

I'm in my room reading something for school and watching a Doris Day movie with the sound off.

Doris Day's real name is Doris Mary Ann von Kappelhoff. Kind of long for anybody's marquee. She was singing with a band and liked a number called "Day by Day," so that's how she got her name.

I don't even know the title of this particular movie. It's one of those not-till-we're-married things with Rock Hudson. She did a bunch of those and got herself called the World's Oldest Virgin. A title I thought I'd hold until Colleen came along.

I hear one little tap on my door, and when I swing around in my fancy desk chair, there's Colleen, standing in my doorway wearing one of my shirts, and on the TV there's Doris Kappelhoff looking coy in Rock Hudson's shirt.

I love that! One girl on a soundstage in Hollywood fifty years ago, the other in South Pasadena right now. Art and Life.

I used to think Art was better, but not anymore.

She pads barefoot across the room and sits on my bed. She takes in the computer, then the big globe on its stand, the movie posters on the walls. Everything always spotless. Spick-and-span. She says, "This place is nicer than a Motel Six."

"Thicker towels, for sure."

"My mom would love that bathtub." She points

toward the spare room. "Nothing but a shower in the last couple of places we've lived." She rubs her arms, pushing up the sleeve of my shirt. "What was in the bubble bath?"

"I don't know. Grandma buys all that stuff."

"I should find out and tell my mom. All she thinks about is how pretty she is. She still works out every day. When I was little, like, five, she was pissed because I was, like, a thousand times more perfect than she could ever be and I didn't have to do anything."

"Was she dancing at clubs then?"

Colleen shakes her head. "Waitressing but going to dance class all the time and sometimes to cattle calls for jobs that paid zip when she got them."

"Where was your dad?"

"Who knows? Probably on a motorcycle somewhere. But she's never alone for long. She had this longtime boy-friend once and she let him watch while she gave me a bath."

I glance at her, but she's staring out the window. "It freaked me out at first, but he never did anything except put the toilet seat down and sit there and smoke, so I got used to it. They'd chat and he'd smoke and I'd try to drown my fuckin' ducky and that was that.

"When I got into my pajamas after dinner, he'd come in, tell me a story, listen to me say my prayers, and then give me ten dollars. Then he'd say, 'You looked like an angel. You're perfect.'"

"Were you scared?"

"Not exactly scared."

"Even when he was looking at you in the bathtub?"

She shrugs. "I felt burgled but not, you know, violated."

Burgled. I was never not in love with her, but that one word lit me up all over again. There's so much more to her than anybody ever sees. I feel like I'm the only one who knows.

I watch her close the blinds and collapse on the bed again.

"You all right?" I ask.

"Sure."

She's flat on her back, hands locked behind her head like a guy in an ad for hammocks. "So," she says, "you get all this eventually, right? The house. The jewels and gold doubloons. You get it all someday."

I tell her, "I guess. Grandma gives a lot of money away."

That makes her sit up so she can see me better, and I wonder if she needs glasses. And if she does, will she bother to go to an eye doctor? And if she goes, how will she pay for them?

"Gives it away to who?" she asks.

"Places that need money. United Way, Project Angel Food, Doctors Without Borders. Places like that."

"Hey, I'm not a doctor, but I'm without a ton of shit. Why doesn't she give me some?"

Just then Grandma calls me from another room. "Ben? Are you decent?"

I say, "Come on in. We're just watching TV." On the screen is an ad for Friday Night Monster Mash. A creature lurches down a dim hallway, holding its arms out like creatures always do. That's what my grandma thinks Colleen is, but she's totally and completely wrong.

Grandma appears in the door, not really looking at me or Colleen but at a spot somewhere in the air a few feet from the ceiling. Maybe she just doesn't want to think about Colleen's bare legs.

Grandma scowls and says, "Do I have to say that I expect everyone to be on their best behavior? I wouldn't leave the two of you alone if I didn't have Schizophrenia. Dinner's in the refrigerator." Then she looks at Colleen. Finally. "No drugs of any kind. Did Ben tell you?"

"He didn't have to. Thanks for letting me stay here. It won't be for long. My mom'll cool down."

Grandma crosses the room and leans down for one of her famous air kisses. "I'm counting on you, Benjamin."

"Don't worry, Grandma."

Colleen tucks her legs up demurely before she asks, "Mrs. Bancroft? What's it like to be rich?"

Grandma either thinks the question over or pretends to. "Let's just say I would like to be remembered as someone who had the opportunity to help those less fortunate."

"So if I had a big, swollen belly and flies crawling all over my face, would you give me money?"

"An organization I am part of certainly might."

"But if you're just walking along the street, and there I am in person, with my belly and my flies, would you, like, slip me a twenty?"

Grandma shakes her head slowly, then pauses at the door before she exits. "I'd be afraid you'd just spend it on narcotics."

Colleen grins. "'Narcotics.' You're really old-school."

After that she just uses a thumbnail to dig at a callus on one heel. When we hear the front door close, she says, "I'm going to sleep some more, Ben, okay? I've never been anywhere this quiet in my life."

She comes over, kisses me innocently. *Burgled but not violated.* I feel so tender toward her. Protective. Maybe I *am* like my dad, who tried to rescue my mom. So what? If I could save Colleen from one more crappy experience, I totally would.

She honest to God saved my life. She gave me—and this is no bullshit—something to live for. I probably wasn't going to kill myself or anything like that, but I was for sure headed for Hermitville. Odd-Duck Town. Weirdo City. The gimp in that nice house who gets ten Netflix deliveries a day and only comes out at night.

She stepped into my life that time at the Rialto, and I started to look forward to waking up in the morning.

* * *

When six o'clock rolls around and it's time to eat, I lead Colleen into the kitchen. I tell her to sit down and I'll do everything.

The casserole Grandma left just needs a few minutes of nuking. In the fridge is a big salad in a shiny, stainless steel bowl. I get a couple of plates and some silverware and hand all of it to Colleen, who deals the plates out but puts the knife and fork and spoon any old way.

"Ben," she says. "I was just thinking: I really like it here."

I turn around and lean on the counter. She's barefoot, and her toes are pink and clean. Jeans and a T-shirt (with no bra). Clothes that I washed for her.

"So," she adds, "maybe just a modest wedding in Big Sur with a few hundred of our closest friends—A.J., the twins, Rane, and Conrad, for sure. Then, after the honeymoon, we can live right here with Grandma."

"She'll be thrilled." Then I limp over and kiss her hair, which smells like my grandmother's shampoo. When I turn around, she kicks me in the butt. She's barefoot, and it isn't a hard kick, but it's a little too hard for just kidding around. That is so Colleen: she likes me and she kicks me. She's kidding and she's serious. One day she's clean and sober, and the next, who knows?

I test the casserole and decide it's not quite hot

enough. I pour some Perrier, hold up the bottle, and watch her shake her head.

She looks around the kitchen before she asks, "Did you talk to the refrigerator when you were little?"

I just look at her. "No."

"That's when I knew I was in trouble. When the refrigerator stopped talking to me."

"What'd it say?"

"Just stuff. Not even about being cold or anything. Mostly, *You're a good girl,* or, *The sun likes you a lot.* Then I'd put my face against it. You didn't do that?"

"No."

"Well, I did, and when I stopped, it hit me like a ton of bricks that I wasn't a good girl and the sun didn't give a rat's ass about me. I was just a little kid with dirty feet, living in a stupid apartment with her stupid mother."

"Mine was just brick by brick, not all at once."

She glances up at me. "Your what was just brick by brick?"

"What you just said. When all of a sudden you know what things are really like. So, when I'm really little I'm in the hospital and back and forth to doctors, and I know that's not normal. But when I'm at home, I still play with other kids, except they can get up and run around and I can't. As long as we're doing board games, I'm fine; then they get skateboards and scooters, and I'm out of it again, right? Brick by brick, see?"

"So you built a little house nobody could blow down, no matter how hard they huffed and puffed."

I nod. "I guess."

"Did you and your folks live here?"

I take a sip of water before I answer. I don't like to think about staring out the window at the other kids, on their skateboards and bikes. "We had a house on Diamond Avenue. I didn't come here until later."

"You mean *we*?"

"I mean *I*. Mom left me on the porch. It was my grandma's porch, but she still left me."

She sits up straighter. "Was the Diamond house nice?"

"It was just a house."

She polishes a clean fork on her T-shirt, then says, "So you moved up, and now you're quite the catch for the right girl: cute, rich, hot to trot."

"Short, crippled, clumsy. You're the only girl who ever looked twice at me."

The microwave pings. I make even lines in the casserole, the way Grandma taught me. Colleen passes the plates. Each one gets a perfect square of quick-and-easy cheesy pasta-and-bean casserole. Then some salad, which has a few candied walnuts and those cherry-size tomatoes. Grandma knows I like candied walnuts.

Colleen starts to eat, but I stay on my feet and pour us big glasses of Alta Dena Dairy's finest.

She puts away most of her dinner in about a minute, then drinks all the milk. I want to ask her when was the last time she ate, but I don't want to sound like her mother. Well, not *her* mother, but a mother.

When she puts the glass down, she has that inevitable white mustache. I know how that would look on film, but I've thought about what Marcie said, and I'm pretty sure she's right. Enough people have used Colleen. She doesn't need one more.

"So, was your mother certifiable?" she asks.

"I don't think she was crazy. Grandma says just fragile."

She takes a last bite—a big one—of casserole, then asks, "Where is she now, anyway?"

I shake my head. "Don't know and don't care. She drove over here one morning about twelve years ago, walked me up to the door, rang the bell, and ran."

She nods. "Wow. Kids do that with a flaming sack of dog shit. Where was your dad?"

"At work. And she's treating me like a flaming sack of dog shit. Why should I want to find her?"

"Lots of reasons: you could ask her why she did what she did. You could see if she's a better person now. You could hit her with a two-by-four."

I reach for a knife I don't need. "Let's just eat dinner and watch a movie, okay?"

"Whatever." She picks at the last of her casserole.

"Did I ever tell you about my adventures with Mom? I'm a toddler. Three years old. Couple of times a week, we go out about six thirty, Mom and me. Get in the car, cruise around till we find a nice neighborhood like this. Park and get out. She'd walk and I'd toddle because . . ." She looks at me expectantly.

"You're a toddler?"

"Exactly. I'm a toddler. Cute as a bug. Walk and toddle, walk and toddle. Finally it starts to get dark, and we're pretty much alone, so she leads me into the bushes beside some awesome house and lifts me up so I can see the people eating dinner or watching TV. Eating off real plates and chatting about fucking *Masterpiece Theatre*. She'd say, 'This is us pretty soon, sweetheart.' Then we'd go eat at Wendy's, where she'd lean over and let the assistant manager look down her dress so he'd super-size us for free. Nice, huh?"

There's sorbet for dessert. Colleen watches me use this special scoop that somehow glides through the hardest ice cream.

She says, "Amazing. Mom and I eat it right out of the carton."

I start to rinse the plates and glasses and put them in the dishwasher. Grandma has a pricey little AM/FM radio on the counter. It (the radio, not the counter) was designed by Jonas Damon. Whoever that is. But it means something to my grandmother. Tonight when I switch it on, Mexican music pours out. The housecleaners probably found that station. Unless my grandma has a secret life.

"Well, aren't you romantic," Colleen says. "All we need is a candle and an extra-large condom."

She can still make me blush. I limp back toward the table. "Should I turn it off?"

"What you should do," she says, "is kiss me."

I lean toward her, but in a way I have to lean through the music, because it's that melancholy. She takes hold of my hair and pulls, but it's not one of her famous collision kisses for a change. It's just a nice kiss.

"I know this song," she says, letting me go like a fisherman doing catch-and-release. "Paloma is a dove and some guy's soul, too. He's crying and not eating, and even the sky is shaking because he's suffering so much for some girl." She finishes my milk in one gulp. "Or some bullshit like that."

"How do you know all that?"

"I ran with some tough chicks. But, you know, mostly on the surface, with the tats and the scars and the stretch marks. The guys are in the other room, doing shots and measuring their dicks, and we're in the kitchen, seeing who's the superskank. But pretty soon we get tired of that, and they start talking about a nice house where they could let their kids play outside and not get clipped by some moron with a piece. And this song comes on, and they start whispering about some *chico* in the sixth grade who wrote poetry."

Her voice has dropped, there's that light on her face (those killer cheekbones), and she's fiddling with the napkin.

I ask, "Did you ever cry over a guy?"

She acts like I'd asked her to recite "The Raven" in Urdu. "Fuck, no. Did you ever cry over a girl?"

"Get serious. I never had a girlfriend to cry over."

"And now you've got two."

I reach for her silverware. "If you mean A.J., first of all, you said she was just curious about me, and you're right. Second, no way would you let me call you my girlfriend."

She looks toward the ceiling and pretends to be amazed. "From Mary Fivefingers — and that doesn't really count — to two live girls. It's like you won the lottery, Ben. Or at least got a second car. Except I'm the beater all corroded by the elements, and A.J.'s a Lexus."

"You're not a corroded beater."

She tucks her head. "Well, I feel like one sometimes."

She lets me smooth her hair and kiss her on dumb places like her shoulders and her nose before we settle in the den, where the big TV is. Barely bigger, actually, than the other ones in the house. My grandma is kind of a semi-Buddhist: she's not attached to large things. So I don't switch on some 102-inch, throbbing plasma, just a supercrisp 32-inch wide-screen LCD.

"What are we watching, baby?"

Baby. It doesn't mean anything. She probably called all her boyfriends *baby.* But I still love it.

I tell her, "It's a surprise."

I've seen *The Usual Suspects* a dozen times. It's a terrific movie, but especially the opening: the dark water, the explosions, the shadowy figure, the guns.

After that, I watch Colleen watch. She's totally absorbed, and that's the expression I love: her mouth open a little while she tries to figure out what everybody else is trying to figure out—who is Keyser Söze?

We work our way through the lineup (that's where the title comes from, which is ironic, because no way are those five guys the usual suspects), the slick robbery, the bungled one, all the way back to the burning ship. Then Verbal Klint, played by the amazing Kevin Spacey, exits the police station dragging one foot and favoring one arm, like he has in every frame until now. But a block away, suddenly he stands straighter and strides out. His left hand unclenches and he lights a cigarette with a gold lighter before he's whisked away in a black Jaguar. The end. Roll credits. Bring up the lights.

Colleen bounces on the couch, she's so jazzed. "Holy shit, Ben. No wonder you love this movie. You are Verbal Klint!"

"Except I'm not pretending to be crippled."

"I'm not saying you don't have C.P. I'm just saying, for years you fooled everybody into thinking you're this total cipher. But you and I go to clubs, you made a movie and showed up at that gallery, and half the school knows who you are now." She pats the cushion right beside her. "Get your disabled ass over here so I can drive you crazy with desire."

But all we do is make out. A little. And that winds down fairly fast. I can tell Colleen's not really into it. Or into me, maybe.

I ask her, "Everything okay?"

She stretches. Her long arms go straight up, and under the one right next to me is a couple of days' worth of stubble. "I'm probably just tired," she says. "I'm not used to all this."

"What's 'all this'?"

"You know — a bathroom all my own, clean sheets, dinner and a movie. It kind of wears me out." She gets to her feet so fast that, even though I'm sitting down, I still lose my balance and fall over on the couch. She says, "I'll see you in the morning, kid."

Three seconds later I'm all by myself, so it's okay for me to roll off the couch, onto the floor, get on my knees, and eventually pull myself up. Not a pretty sight.

I'm barely in my bedroom before the phone rings, and it's A.J.

"Is this too late? Were you asleep?"

"No, it's okay. What's up?"

"Did you get my message about the racetrack? Well, my dad set it up, but it's for tomorrow morning. Are you okay with that?"

"Sure."

"Six a.m. tomorrow morning."

"Yikes."

"So . . . ?"

"What if Colleen came with us? I don't think she'll want to, but what if she did?"

There's a very long three-second silence before A.J. asks, "Why would she want to?"

"She's staying here. With Grandma and me. For just a couple of days."

"And this is just you being a good friend?"

"Something like that. Nobody ever crashed at your house?"

"Yeah, but we made s'mores and watched DVDs."

"She doesn't have anyplace else to go."

"What about her parents?"

"Out of the picture or hopeless."

"Are you serious?" A.J. asks. "She's totally on her own?"

"Pretty much. She's a tough cookie."

"Tell me about it."

* * *

In the morning, Grandma finds me in the kitchen.

"Benjamin, are you all right? What are you doing up so early?"

I'd been staring at the All-Bran box, and it was staring back. "I'm fine. A.J. and I are going to that racetrack in Arcadia."

"Neither one of you is old enough to bet."

"Grandma, it's still dark. Nobody's betting. It's just when we can talk to this jockey for this movie A.J. thinks she wants to make."

Grandma's wearing a nightgown and something that matches over that. They're both filmy, and I'd never tell her this, but she looks a little like one of Dracula's wives. When I was little, I thought she slept standing up so nothing would get wrinkled.

"Is Colleen asleep?" she asks.

"Everybody's asleep but you and me and a bunch of jockeys."

"Is Colleen going with you and your new friend?"

"I'll ask, but there's no way. Colleen's not a morning person."

She looks at the coffeepot on the stove but doesn't get up. I tell her, "I'll get it for you."

"No, caffeine makes me meditate too fast." She adjusts the salt and pepper shakers, lining them up perfectly. "When Colleen does wake up, what should I do with her? I'm going to yoga."

"She knows where the kitchen is."

"But she'll be here alone."

I pick up the bowl and drink the last of the milk. Grandma hates it when I do that. "She's not going to steal the silver."

"Oh, Benjamin. I know that."

I stand up and put my napkin on the chair like I might come back. "My mom had a job, right?"

Grandma looks up at me. "Why this sudden interest in your mother?"

"I don't know. Colleen and I were swapping stories last night. So, did my mom have a job? I kind of remember her being dressed up when she dropped me off here for the day."

"Before your father was killed, she'd managed to get her real-estate license."

"So she sold houses."

"She showed a house or two, but that was the extent of it."

"She was pretty, wasn't she?"

Grandma takes what I'm sure her yoga teacher would call a deep, cleansing breath. "She was."

Except for my cereal bowl, the table is spotless, and there's a rose in a little crystal vase. I know what Colleen meant last night about all this wearing her out. It's so picture-perfect. Maybe that's why I like documentaries. They're almost always rough around the edges.

"So she—" But I don't get to finish because there's the lightest, most polite *tap-tap* at the front door.

I ask, "Do you want to say hi to A.J.?"

"Just say that I'll call her mother later about the Congo."

I let A.J. in, ask her to wait one minute, then go to Colleen's room. I knock until I hear her move around and then go in. She sits up and squints at me.

"What time is it?"

"About five thirty."

She collapses. "Oh, my God!"

"I'm going out with A.J. for a little while. Movie stuff. You can come if you want."

Colleen just turns over and mutters, "Tell her to keep her fuckin' hands to herself. You're mine."

I close the door carefully, nod to A.J., and we head for her car.

"Colleen not coming?" she asks.

I point to the barely light sky. "Too early for her."

A.J. signals just coming out of the driveway. We make our way down Mission, past the park, with its spotless playground. Parents pay big bucks to live someplace they can take the kids to a teeter-totter and a sandbox and not have to worry too much.

"Grandma says for you to tell your mom she'll call her about the Congo." And Colleen says for you to keep your f**king hands to yourself. What would A.J. say if I tacked that on? Laugh, probably. But what would I do if she didn't keep her hands to herself?

We cruise through the first two stoplights, but not the next one. Ten feet away, at a local nursery, a Hispanic guy in thrashed blue Dickies trundles two or three flats of pansies toward a big SUV with its back standing open like Moby Dick's jaws. The driver, who's pretty and clearly super-rich—since I've never seen the nursery open so early—is standing off to the side in a sun hat and dainty leather gloves.

I ask, "Do you want to be rich?"

She takes her eyes off the road just long enough to glance at me. "When I grow up?"

"You know what I mean."

She oozes around an Escalade waiting to park in three or four compact-car spaces. I notice she's dressed for the racetrack. Not the jeans. Everybody wears jeans, even me. But boots and a shirt with snaps. I wonder if she's got a cowboy hat in the back.

"I either want to go to the International Film School in Paris or to the New York Film Academy. I'd work if I had to. Be a waitress or something."

"When we were talking down at that gallery, you said USC."

"I know, but my mom and I were online, poking into things, and Paris or New York sounds better."

"Then what?"

"Make more movies. Better ones. And my father knows the Coppolas."

"Colleen doesn't know where she'll be sleeping two days from now."

"Are you worried about her?"

"Sure. Wouldn't you be?"

We wind through the wide streets of San Marino. Shiny cars in a few of the driveways. A gardener or two. Huge homes, the kind my grandma would call "tasteful," compared to the McMansions springing up in Monterey Park and Alhambra.

The lawns are beautiful and huge. And there's usually a pool with turquoise water that nobody but the grandkids use and when they're grown, nobody at all.

I tell A.J., "I've been in a lot of these houses. Grandma used to bring me along when she had meetings and park me in the den with the TV. Every now and then a maid would ghost in and ask me if I wanted anything."

A.J. asks, "Have you guys got a maid?"

I shake my head.

"Do you have somebody who comes in and cleans?"

"Yeah, but I never see them. They do it while I'm at school."

"My mom works at JPL and cleans our whole house, too. Can you believe that? She's really picky. If Merry Maids or one of those services comes in, it's never good enough for her. So she just does it herself."

Huntington Drive is pretty much the main drag of San Marino. It's named for Henry Huntington, a megarich guy whose name is everywhere in L.A. Like Huntington Beach and Huntington Hospital.

The street runs east and west and eventually right into a mall. Just northeast of that a little is the racetrack. A.J. turns in and zips across an empty parking lot, scattering seagulls. She pulls up beside a guard shack on the west side of the huge, deco-green grandstand.

While she talks, I look out the window. A few guys who are too big to be jockeys ride along a dirt path. Their horses look healthy and sleek and relaxed. The riders' feet dangle out of the stirrups. They talk to each other and laugh under their breath. Off to the east, the sky is Technicolor red.

Everything is muffled and low-key. Probably not like later on, when they run the races. I've seen the Kentucky Derby on TV, and it's a madhouse. But not now.

A.J. thanks the guard and aims for a parking space a hundred yards away. Then we amble — well, A.J. does — toward another guard shack.

"I've got an appointment to see Blake Edwards," she says.

The guard points a big, pockmarked nose at a clipboard. He picks up a phone with one hand and hands us two passes with the other. "Tear off the backs and stick 'em on your clothes somewheres."

They say BACKSTRETCH VISITOR, then there's the date. A.J. puts hers on her shirt, and I do, too.

"You all can go on in a ways," the guard says. "Blake's comin'."

Green barns stretch beyond where we are and off to the left and right. They're a little like barracks, just with lots of doors. The Dutch kind, with a top half and a bottom half that can open on its own. There's no concrete or asphalt, just raked dirt. Horses look out of their stalls or are led around by somebody. Guys mostly, but some girls, too.

A.J. tells us, "My dad says this is your whole world if you want it to be. They've got doctors back here; you can go to the dentist, buy clothes, even take classes."

A lanky guy on horseback stops beside us. Black boots and jeans. A black muscle shirt, black leather vest. Black hair. All he needs is a mask, and he's Zorro.

"Pretty lady," he croons to A.J. "You should never have to walk anywhere. Let me take you wherever you want to go."

She looks up at him. "I'm fine right where I am, thank you."

"You're visiting," he says. "I'm visiting, too. Maybe we can visit together."

"Go feed your horse," she says. "He looks hungry."

He leans toward her, and all kinds of leather creak. "Just so you know — merely the sight of you has made this day special." Then he clucks to his horse and spurts away.

A.J. glances at me. "Let's hope they're not all like that."

Somebody — a kid about my age and for sure shorter than me — heads for us. He's in jeans, too, and low-heeled boots. There's a heavy, protective vest over a T-shirt. He's wearing a helmet, which he takes off as he stops beside us and holds out his hand. I don't know what I expected, but Blake Edwards looks like a ninth-grader. Smooth, round cheeks. Tan, bare arms but not all muscled up. He's got bad teeth, and he knows it, because he pretends to cough a lot so he can cover his mouth.

"I guess you're A.J."

I shake my head. "I'm Ben. This is A.J."

"Oh."

I tell him, "You're named after a famous movie director."

"Oh, yeah? Who's that?"

"Blake Edwards."

He shakes his head. "Don't know him."

A.J. points. "Can we talk over there by those hay bales?"

Blake shrugs. "I guess."

A.J. explains her idea for the documentary. Different from that *Jockeys* show on Animal Planet. No romance. No rivalries. Just deep, probing interviews.

Blake puts one heel in the dirt and grinds at it. "I don't know."

"What don't you know?" she asks.

He looks down at the ground and scowls. "I just don't know."

I follow A.J. and Blake. She gets the background she wants (enough barn and hay, enough space for a horse to walk through the frame) and lifts the camera she's been toting in a black bag. A camera bigger than mine. Pricier.

"You're leading rider out here, correct?" she asks.

"Nope."

"I thought . . . My dad said you were."

"Nope." He looks at me. "Leading apprentice rider."

"What's that like?" A.J. asks.

"Okay, I guess."

"Is it dangerous, riding Thoroughbred horses?"

Blake snorts. "What do you think?"

A.J. glances in my direction. She lets her camera dangle at arm's length. "Is there a bathroom around here?" she asks.

Blake points. A.J. hands me the Sony. Her eyes—as they say in cheese-o novels—meet mine. Not in a romantic way, though. This is business. "I'll be back in a minute."

When she's too far away to hear, Blake says, "She your girlfriend?"

"Uh-uh."

"Have you got a girlfriend?"

"Kind of." I swing the camera up and point it. "What about you?"

"Long as I've got five hundred dollars in my pocket, I'm six feet tall with a bright future. You know what rodeo is?"

"Sure."

"In rodeo there's girls called buckle bunnies. They only go with guys who win prizes. There's like that in horse racing, too. Those kind of girls."

"Nobody you'd want to take home to Mama, I guess."

"Shit, my momma was like that." He points to the camera. "Is that thing on?"

I lie. "I'm just playing with the focus and the light and stuff." I pretend to fiddle with the camera. "But you're winning prizes now, right?"

He nods. "Money, yeah. But I'll tell you, man, it's not *if* I'm gonna go down and break something. It's just when and how bad. Every now and then some poor son of a bitch in a wheelchair comes back here, and I think, *That could be me.*" Blake steps closer. "I'm goin' thirty miles an hour on an animal that weighs about two thousand pounds. All around me is six or seven other guys who'd just as soon put me over the rail as look at me, 'cause every race I win is food off their table."

"Sounds tough."

"Between you an' me? It's a total nightmare. Get

up at four a.m., eat half a piece of toast, drive out here and work horses for guys who might or might not ever give you a leg up. Sleep a little, then put on some stupid-lookin' silk shirt and get on a horse that'd just as soon step on me as look at me." He points, and I know what he's pointing at. What everybody always, sooner or later, points at. "What happened to you, anyway?"

"Something went haywire in my brain right after I was born. You can't catch it."

"You sound like your brain's okay."

"It is, but not the rest of me."

"Are you gonna be all right?"

"I'm all right now."

"You go to school and all that?"

"High school, yeah."

He nods. "I'm stupid. Everybody always told me I was, so I guess I am. I'm lucky I can do this. You don't have to be smart to hold on."

"It takes more than just holding on to be leading anything, and you're the best apprentice, right?"

He coughs and puts one hand over his mouthful of bad teeth. "Lookit," he says, "I got to work a horse for this guy. This interview thing isn't goin' anywhere. I just did it 'cause a guy who knows a guy told me I ought to. I'm gonna tell him it just didn't work out, okay?"

"Sure."

We shake hands again, and he hurries away.

A.J., who's been lurking around the nearest corner, starts toward me.

"I didn't have to pee," she says. "I thought maybe he'd open up to you."

"I know. I got a couple of minutes' worth." I hand her the camera. I watch her watch until she says, "Wow. How'd you do that?"

"A guy thing, probably. But that's all we're gonna get."

"Are you sure?" She taps the camera. "This is great."

"He's kind of a miniature chauvinist. He won't talk to you."

"That's okay. You talk to him. You get, like, tons of footage, and I'll edit it. We'll put both our names on it."

I help her pack up the camera. I like talking about this. She's not just a cute rich girl from the right side of the tracks, and I'm not just a spaz. We're filmmakers with problems that filmmakers have. Problems we can probably solve. The minute I picked up the camera, I stopped thinking about anything else.

We trudge toward the stable gate. I'm tired and my hip hurts. Big pickups driven by little men filter out of the gate.

In the parking lot, the seagulls she'd scared driving in are standing around her car.

"All we need is Rod Taylor," she says.

"And Tippi Hedren."

"And Suzanne Pleshette."

"And let's not forget the great Jessica Tandy."

We're talking in shorthand about Hitchcock's *The Birds.*

As she unlocks a back door and we stow the gear, she says, "My dad's kind of like Rod Taylor was in that movie." She looks at me. "His name was Mitch, right?"

"Mitch Brenner."

"A little cold. No funny business: *Let's board up those windows and block the fireplace.* So Mom and I are Jessica Tandy and Suzanne Pleshette, just hanging around, waiting for crumbs of affection." She fiddles with her keys. "Too much information?"

I shake my head. "No."

She loops around to the driver's side. I climb in and put on the seat belt. But when it looks like we're good to go, she doesn't start the car.

"This is none of my business, Ben, but . . ." She studies the speedometer. "Are you and Colleen together?"

Was that a snowman driving that bus?

Did that nun just drink a bucket of brine?

That's the line reading she gave her question: Stupefied. Amazed. Maybe even impressed. She can barely get her mind around it. That Colleen would like me. Would want to be with me. Or that I would want to be with her, maybe. Or that I even could.

I tell her the truth, some of it, anyway. "She's just staying with Grandma and me a couple of days."

"But are you together?"

"Sometimes."

A.J. puts the key in the ignition. Her key chain has a little LED light on it for those dark nights outside the mansion. That, and a little two-inch bear. She leans against the steering wheel. Puts her head on it like she's sleepy.

"I'm kind of with Conrad," she says. "I don't know why. We never have any fun. And he's either just mean or super-careless and totally self-absorbed. Like, he'll call me on Friday and say he wants to do something. I've got plans but I cancel them. Then he doesn't show up. So I watch anything on TV and eat bag after bag of Cheetos." She turns my way. "How stupid is that?"

She leans toward me, one hand out. I start to give her my gimpy one, the runty one, the ugly one. Then I remember that only Colleen touches me all over. So I bring my right hand across.

A.J. half whispers, "You and I just made kind of a good team in there, that's all." She puts her other hand on mine, covers it up with both of hers like it's a little fire she's trying to keep alive. And then she leans some more and kisses me.

Thanks to Colleen, I know how to kiss, but it's nothing like that. It's okay, though, and I'm flattered and curious. Somebody else's lips — amazing!

But this kiss never goes anywhere. It doesn't get

warmer or messier. It's the kind of kiss that would just put Snow White into a deeper coma.

There I am with a cute girl who likes me, at least a little. We're into some of the same things. Or at least the same big thing—movies. I don't have to worry about getting arrested; she's not going to run off with some stranger and smoke a joint. A.J. swears about once a month, and her skin, at least what I can see of it, is a perfect, blank canvas. And when Grandma sees her, she doesn't make a face.

So why am I thinking about Colleen?

WHEN A.J. DROPS ME OFF, it's about ten. Grandma's car is gone. Colleen isn't outside, but she's not in her bedroom or the bathroom or any other room. I'm just about to call her cell when she bursts through the front door.

"Big news!" she says. "Huge news. I found your mother!"

All I can do is stare.

"And I'm staying with Marcie for a while, but that's nothing."

"My mother is at Marcie's?" I gasp.

"No, she's in Azusa!" She holds an envelope right in front of my eyes, and I read Grandma's address and then, up in the left-hand corner, hers:

> **Delia Bancroft**
> **111-D Magnolia**
> **Azusa, CA 91702**

"Where . . . ?" I'm having trouble catching my breath. Colleen takes my face in both hands and kisses me. Breathes into me. Makes me breathe. It's not sexy; it's resuscitation. Finally I can wheeze, "Where did you find this?"

"In your grandma's bedroom."

"What were you doing in there?"

"Snooping around. You don't look in people's medicine cabinets when you go to their houses?"

I point the envelope at her. "This wasn't in Grandma's medicine cabinet."

"So it was on her desk."

"She doesn't leave stuff on her desk."

"In a drawer, then. Jesus. What's the difference? Now we can find your mother and beat her up." She grabs my good hand and tugs.

"Now?"

"Sure."

"We can't just go out there."

"Why not?"

"We just can't."

"Do you want some guy in gold pants and a trumpet to announce your arrival?"

"She doesn't know we're coming."

"We'll catch her off guard. See the real her." She pulls at me and I let her.

"This is crazy."

"I don't know about you, Ben, but I can't wait to see the heartless bitch who left you on Granny's doorstep like a sack of flaming dog shit. I'll leave Grandma a note."

"Since when are you so concerned about my grandma?"

"Since we had breakfast together about an hour ago. She's kind of a cool old lady."

Colleen crosses the double lines and gets into the carpool lane of the 210 freeway. I tell her, "I don't feel too good."

She glances over, a cigarette dangling from her lips. Colleen smokes like somebody in a gangster film, the tough chick who gets killed in a shoot-out so the misunderstood hoodlum can marry the pretty librarian.

I take a few deep breaths as we whiz past Monrovia. I want to think about anything except where we're going. "So how did you end up at Marcie's?"

She takes one last drag on her cigarette and flicks it

away. It carries and makes an arc of showering sparks. Robert Mitchum couldn't have done it better.

"I called a few people I know, and in that warm-hearted way of drug addicts everywhere, they told me to get lost. So I go out to my car, where I think I've got some more phone numbers, and there's Marcie, working in the yard. She asks me how I'm doing, one thing leads to another, and the next thing you know, I've got the Virginia Woolf suite. So I'm set for a little while." She reaches over and rubs my face. "Now we'll find your mom and tie up a few loose ends, okay?"

We blow by the Baldwin off-ramp, the one A.J. and I took just a few hours ago when we left the racetrack. I think about her life, all planned out, starting with Paris or New York. How she said we made a good team. That lukewarm kiss in the parking lot.

Colleen and I ride for a while. People check us out, guys, mostly. Alone in their cars with fifty-two payments to go. They're wearing their nice shirts and ties. They're on their way to shake somebody's limp hand. I'll bet they're thinking, *I wish I was in high school again. I wish I was that guy.*

I tell her, "My alleged mother probably isn't going to be home. You know that, don't you?"

"So we'll come back."

"She could be food shopping or working or out with friends."

"Did she have friends before? Did she have a job?"

"I don't remember. Grandma says she had a real-estate license but never sold anything."

"Relax. We'll do some recon: find her house, check out her car. If she's got four or five Mexicans in the trunk, she's a smuggler."

"Even if she is home, I can't just go to the door and say, 'Hello, I'm your son,' then throw my one good arm around her and weep."

"Why not?"

"Colleen, she doesn't want to see me, not really. If she wanted to see me, she would. We live twenty miles away from each other, okay? Maybe that's all I want to do today — see her. Just look at her."

"Fine. So we'll take a look at her. But don't forget: you live twenty miles away from each other *now*. What's that note say again?"

I open the envelope and read out loud:

> Dear Mrs. Bancroft,
>   Thank you for the money. It cost more to
> move and get situated than I planned. My new
> address is on the envelope.
>   Yours,
>   Delia Bancroft

Colleen says, "See? She's getting situated. She might've moved to be closer to you."

"And today's prize for unbridled optimism goes to the lady in the blue Vans, Colleen Minou."

Colleen careens across three lanes, exits way too fast, slides around the corner, and finally comes to a stop at a big intersection with a barbecue joint on one corner and a Chevron station across the street.

"You're the worst driver I've ever seen."

"Ed and I used to have to run from the Mexican mafia."

"You should be making movies, not me."

Colleen looks both ways a couple of times. Then lights a cigarette.

I suggest, "Want to ask at the gas station?"

"Look at the Thomas Guide. It's down there under all those In-N-Out Burger wrappers."

I find it and pry the sticky pages apart. Colleen's arm is across the back of my seat, rubbing my shoulder. A.J. could drive me out here. Or Grandma or even Rane, but they couldn't keep me from just jumping out of the car and running right back the way we came. Colleen knows me. She really knows me.

I tell her, "Looks like left here a couple of blocks and then right on Magnolia."

"Good work, Magellan. Now let's go and find your mommy."

Two blocks and one turn later, we come to Magnolia and then to 111. My mother—how weird are those two words? — lives in a court. Not a trailer court, thank God. Little units, six on a side, fill up a deep lot. Not like the three-story building next door with a hundred apartments that hogs the sun.

One eleven is a little seedy, like in *Day of the Locust*, the ultimate movie about Hollywood the way it used to be. The light that falls on it looks like weak tea. The kind you might make for a sick person, and then add a piece of toast cut into a triangle.

Colleen peers from across the street. "So if she's in D, and I can see A from here, she's in the fourth one up on the left."

There's one uncomfortable-looking chair on the tiny porch.

We just sit. Colleen smokes. I take deep breaths and let them out with a *whoosh*. Finally I say, "If this was a movie and we were staking this place out, she'd open the door and walk straight to her car. They never show the twelve hours the cops sat there drinking coffee."

Colleen points. "Bingo!"

Somebody comes out of unit D. Somebody in a blouse and skirt. Carrying a purse and one of those little insulated lunch bags.

My heart rate shoots up.

Colleen slaps me on the arm. "Am I gonna have to call the paramedics?"

I shake my head. "Oh, my God. Is that her?"

We watch her walk toward the street, eyes down. Her hair is stringy, still damp from a shower, probably.

I gasp. "She's kind of fat. She didn't used to be fat."

"Yeah, she hasn't been going to the gym much, that's for sure. And she's not smuggling illegal aliens, either. Coyotes make a lot of money."

She gets into an old Sentra. The blinker comes on, she looks over her shoulder, then pulls away from the curb.

"Driver," Colleen says to herself, "follow that car."

We make our way down Azusa Avenue, tailing my mother's dusty Nissan.

I tell myself over and over: *That's your mother in that car. Your actual mother.*

I point. "Wait. Look. She's slowing down."

"How can you tell? If she drives any slower, we'll be parked."

But she doesn't stop. She's just super-cautious. A quarter of a block away, there's a mom with a four-year-old, standing on the curb and talking into her cell. My mom acts like the kid might dart into the street.

We speed up a whole five miles per hour. Colleen lights another cigarette.

"Why do you smoke so much?" I ask her.

"Oral fixation." She waggles her eyebrows at me.

"That'd be a lot sexier if you didn't look like Groucho Marx."

I glance around. Azusa looks like the kind of place that's semiclose to places that are actually close to Disneyland or L.A. or the beach. There's a row of motels like Super 8 and Best Western. In the parking lots, people who travel slightly off season to save money pack up the minivans and yell at their kids.

We pass signs for a country club, a river trail, and the Burro Canyon Shooting Park.

Colleen points. "I think I was out here with Ed once. He wanted me to know how to use a handgun in case things got dicey in the marijuana business."

"Remember 'Liar, liar, pants on fire'?"

She glances down. "These are new pants, too."

"Why do you think my mom picked this place to live?"

"Why does anybody do anything? It's cheap. That little shack of hers would be called a charming cottage in South Pasadena, and it'd go for thirteen hundred a month. I'll bet it's not eight out here in the middle of nowhere."

I adjust the bucket hat Grandma wants me to wear so I won't get skin cancer. "So she moves down here from God knows where, finds a cheap place to live, drives twenty-two miles an hour and signals four blocks before she wants to turn. What's up with her?"

"We'll trap her in a corner. You cry and yell at her for leaving you on Grandma's doorstep, and every now and then I'll ask, 'And by the way, why do you drive so slow?'"

I look over at Colleen. I put my sick hand on the wheel, right beside hers. "I'm glad you're here. I couldn't do this without you."

"Ah, bullshit. You totally could. It just wouldn't be as much fun." Colleen slows to a crawl. "Heads up," she says. "I think we've reached our destination."

The Sentra turns into a big parking lot beside a Target store. Shoppers with red carts cross in front of us.

"There's some smart gals," Colleen says. "You never know when you're going to need a hundred rolls of toilet paper."

When the Sentra oozes all the way to the farthest corner of the lot, we slide in between two SUVs.

"I'll bet she works here," Colleen says. "They always want their minimum-wage lackeys to leave the primo spaces for the customers."

I tell her, "I don't get it. Mom and Dad were married. She should have gotten half of everything."

Colleen opens her door. "C'mon, Hopalong. This crafty varmint's on the move."

My mother walks as slowly as she drives. She clutches her purse with both hands and stays as close to the wall as she can.

We follow her through the big electric doors, past a bored-looking guard wearing what looks like his big brother's uniform. Then she disappears through a door marked EMPLOYEES ONLY.

"What now?" I ask.

"We wait. In the meantime, we pretend to shop. Try and fit in, okay? Walk behind me like all the other guys and look like your balls are in a vise."

Nobody looks very happy. Most of the women have three or four kids grabbing at anything, and Dad's a human calculator wondering what this excursion is going to cost. Spacey-looking tweens text each other as fast as they can.

Colleen links her arm through mine and leads me to a wall of socks, where she pretends to be enthralled with some Hello Kitty knee-highs.

Then she stops abruptly. "Whoa. Look who's here."

It's my mother, in a one-size-fits-none vest. Her brown pants are loose. Black, soft-looking shoes, run down a little like she's heavier on one side. Pale.

"Was she always like that?" Colleen asks.

"Like what?"

"Invisible."

I tell Colleen, "Not to me. We'd go places together. Grandma, too."

"Old laugh-a-minute Granny." She pulls me behind a rack of dresses with flowers all over them. "What'd your dad do, anyway?"

"Remember when we went to Caltech to see Marcie's movie? I showed you the library where Dad worked."

"I thought you guys were rich."

"Grandma is."

"And as far as the C.P. goes, you were pretty much screwed from day one, right?"

"If you want to use abstruse medical terminology, yes."

She leans in and kisses me. "I fuckin' love you, Ben. You just crack me up."

My mother disappears through the wide doors marked CHANGING ROOMS. But only for a few seconds. Then she's back, pushing a cart loaded with all kinds of clothes. Loaded to overflowing. She has to lean to push it, like the coal miners in *How Green Was My Valley*. Or the seven dwarfs in their diamond mine.

We watch her trudge, take a blue dress off the top of the pile, look at the label, then put it back on a rack with a dozen others just like it. She moves like she's underwater.

Colleen says, "It looks like Count Dracula's been stopping by her cottage for snacks. Either that or she's loaded."

I don't mean to, but I take a step back. "I don't know what to do."

"Talk to her. The shock might start her heart."

"What do I say?"

"How about, 'Remember when you dropped me off at Grandma's? Well, I'm still waiting for you to pick me up, and, boy, am I thirsty'?"

"I'm serious, Colleen."

"Okay, okay. Just walk over there and say, 'I think you're my mom. Do you remember me? I'm Ben.'"

I retreat some more. "I can't."

"Then I'll do it."

"NO!"

I've got my hand around her wrist and she uncurls my fingers one by one. "Relax. You just try on one of these whimsical prints with a cinch waist and side pockets."

I watch her walk away. I step in between the long dresses, the ones with the flowers. But they smell like chemicals. Like I'm in a chemical jungle.

Colleen waits until my mother figures out that the white blouse in the cart belongs with the other white blouses. Then Colleen says something. Delia's hands (I can't totally think of her as my mother, so I default to what Grandma calls her) reach for each other. Then they disappear into the sleeves of her blouse. But I can see them moving in there. Turning and twisting. Writhing.

Colleen waves me over. Another deep breath, another big *whoosh,* and I totter toward them.

She doesn't look up, but one hand comes out tentatively. "Benjamin," she whispers. "What a coincidence."

"Yeah," I croak. "Isn't it?"

She looks at Colleen. "What brings you to Azusa?"

"Oh, we were just driving around."

She takes her hand back. Her limp, damp hand. "It's a lovely place to live."

Colleen nods. "It looks nice."

Her face closes down a little. "I need to get back to work. They're always watching. And there's always something to do. I have to keep my area shoppable. I have to zone the junior knits." She points. "And this isn't the only cart I have to attend to."

Colleen smiles reassuringly. "Listen. Do you get a break anytime soon? I could use some caffeine. Any chance of sitting down somewhere?"

My mother checks her watch, a Timex with a cracked leather band. "Just let me get someone to keep an eye on my section."

While she's gone, Colleen says, "So far, so good, right?"

"Here are my choices: I can either faint or throw up."

"Door number one. That way I can give you mouth-to-mouth. No way is that going to happen if you hurl."

We follow Delia toward the cash registers. Past those, I can see a yellow-and-blue room with tables. Grandma would need more than one digestive enzyme to eat here.

My mother's pants are a little off-kilter. Her vest slants the other way. Her too-big brown socks sag a little.

"What would you kids like?" she asks, sounding like she's memorized the line.

Colleen helps me out. "We'll have what you're having."

Delia turns and looks at us slyly. "It's probably not good for us, but it's delicious."

I reach for one of the twenty-dollar bills Grandma gives me. "Let me pay, okay?"

She waves it away, "Oh, that's not necessary, Benjamin."

"I know, but I'd like to."

She lets me lay it across her open hand. "Well, all right. I do get the employee discount."

The girl behind the counter — stud in her nose, blue hair — looks at Colleen and gives up the slightest nod.

My mother says, "You kids should sit down. I can manage."

Colleen and I find a table without too much mustard on it. I tell her, "I just can't believe that's actually my mother."

"We're reading this play in Alternative School where this Oedipus guy sleeps with his mom. So what you are going through here is nothin'."

"Have I told you lately what a great consolation you are in these stressful times?"

She leans into me, flicks her tongue in my ear. "Keep talkin' like that, big boy, and you might get lucky tonight." Then she nudges me. "Uh-oh. Despite what she said, I don't think Mom's coping all that well."

I hurry over. Three corn dogs and three cups of 7-Up are too much for one tray.

I get another one and manage to off-load all the drinks. "Now we've each got one, okay?"

Relief just makes her face light up. I follow her to the table. Colleen, God bless her, stands up and helps with the flimsy red plates, the ketchup and mustard, the plastic knives and forks.

Delia settles in, worries her napkin till it opens and floats onto her lap. And immediately slips off. She reaches for it, but it's too far away. I try, but it's on my left, and that arm is, well, that arm. Colleen simply hands her another one.

My mother looks at me. Actually, at my partly shriveled arm. "Has that been difficult for you, Benjamin?"

"I manage."

"You seem quite capable."

"He's more than capable," Colleen says, with a leer.

Delia acts like she's only heard the content, not the tone. "Well, that's such good news," she says. "I'm glad."

Then she gives all her attention to her corn dog— holding it down with a fork, slowly withdrawing the stick, cutting it into six bite-size pieces.

"These are kosher dogs," she says, "so we don't have to worry about a pig's anus in our lunch."

Colleen pushes her plate away and reaches for the 7-Up.

I take a deep breath. "So, where were you before you moved to Azusa?"

She chews a long time before she answers, and while she's chewing, I wonder if she'll ask how I know she lived somewhere else. If she asks how I know, what do I say? But not much registers with my mother except the basics.

"Seattle," she says. "I was in Seattle."

"No way," Colleen blurts. "Seattle is the fucking suicide capital of the world."

"It could get gloomy," Delia says. "Perhaps that's why my doctor says I needed sunshine. Now I have a comfortable chair on my front porch, and I sit out there all the time."

My corn dog bulges in the middle like a python who's just had his supper.

I manage to ask, "What did you do up in Washington?"

"Oh, I worked."

I really want to know if she left California because I was so much trouble. But I can't ask. Not today, anyway. Not with her hunched over that awful corn dog.

"Do you like the movies?" Colleen asks. "Ben loves the movies."

She pauses and looks up. Her eyes are just like mine — light blue and deepset. God, she's my mother for sure. "I used to," she says, "but I haven't been in years."

I ask, "What kind did you like?"

She moves her fork like a tiny baton. "Where people sang and danced in the streets or around a fountain."

Colleen puts one arm around my waist and pulls me toward her. It's such a cool thing for her to do. I can feel her through our clothes: we're in this together. "This looks like a pretty nice place to work," she says. "Do you like it?"

Her shoulders sag some more. "I'm solely responsible for at least a thousand square yards of ladies' wear." She ticks off brands on one hand. "Liz Lange, Xhilaration, Mossimo, Merona Slimming Solutions. And then there are the UPC numbers."

Thinking about it seems to wear her out. She closes her eyes. Colleen and I look at each other: Did my mother nod out over a corn dog?

Just then somebody else in a Target vest stops, touches Delia on the shoulder, and says, "Who are your friends, honey?"

She's a big, strong woman who radiates energy. She reminds me of Queen Latifah (real name Dana Elaine Owens), who was good in *Chicago* and just won my heart in a little movie called *Last Holiday*.

My mother actually wakes up a little. "Oh, Monique. This is Ben. He's all grown up."

I get to my feet. "We haven't seen each other in a while." I put one hand on Colleen's shoulder and introduce her.

"That's a pretty blouse," Monique says. "You didn't buy that here."

"Fell off the back of a truck headed for New York."

Monique smiles. "Well, I should be getting back. Guess who has to zone men's dress pants?"

Delia checks her watch. She puts both hands flat on the table and is about to push herself to her feet when Colleen says, "Look at this." She grabs my good hand and sets it beside my mother's. They actually are alike.

Then she's on her feet. "Really. I can't be late."

Colleen shoos her. "You go. We'll clean up here."

Delia puts both hands deep into the pockets of her smock: no hugging today. "Well, thank you for coming. I really enjoyed myself."

We watch her walk away. Hurry, really. Or scurry. I take a deep breath and sit down. Colleen thumps the table with one fist. "I think we made some progress today, doctor."

"It's like she doesn't get it. That it's been twelve years. That I'm her kid. Is she ever going to ask about Grandma?"

"Speaking of Ms. Congeniality, when are you going to tell her?"

I shake my head. "That I found my mom? I don't know."

"But you will, right? You have to."

"Eventually."

Colleen digs for her keys, points to the exit. I take her hand, and she leads me away. I'm almost as comatose as my mother.

"Unbelievable," I say once we've cleared the door and are outside again.

"Yeah," she says. "Not like the movies, where Mommy says she's sorry and then the violin section kicks in."

"She hasn't seen her kid for twelve years, he shows up out of nowhere, and she says, 'What a coincidence.'"

"Get in the car, honey. Stop thinking for two minutes."

"She can't be like this all the time, can she?"

"We'll find out, okay? We'll come back. She could be part of a shadowy netherworld of Zombie Moms, at which point we'll have to get out the flamethrower."

I fall into the seat. Colleen reaches across and fastens my seat belt. She kisses me and puts her warm cheek against mine. "It'll be fine. You'll be fine. You're kind of in shock — that's all. Anybody would be."

As Colleen drives, I keep thinking: That's *my mother?* That's *the person I thought about and worried about and, when I was little, anyway, cried myself to sleep over? Holy shit!*

"You okay, sport?"

"I don't know."

"Talk to me. We meet this genie, okay? And we each get three wishes. You know what I'd wish for? Huge boobs. Then you'd never ever want any girl but me. Huge boobs and a movie theater. What would you wish for?"

She leans and pokes me with an elbow. "C'mon. What would you wish for?"

"I know you're trying to distract me. Thanks, but I'm okay."

"Bullshit. I'm really interested. What would you want if you could——?"

"Okay, okay. Fine. Two good arms and legs and a car, okay? That's all. I'd just like to be a regular kid with a car."

Colleen swallows hard. "Well, fuck. Now I'm going to cry."

"I didn't cry back there."

"You totally did. People were staring at you. They were taking pictures. You'll be on YouTube tomorrow—— *Former Orphan Outdoes Niagara.*"

"Will you just stop?"

"Fine." She scans the traffic all around us and mutters. "Like a bunch of salmon going upstream to spawn. Big honkin' mortgages, rug rats in the back, grills on the patio, all the beer they can drink." She shudders, and it doesn't look like she's pretending, either. "Talk about *Night of the Living Dead.*"

"You remember *Night of the Living Dead?*"

She takes her eyes off the road to tell me, "Oh, Ben. I remember every second of every movie we ever saw together."

* * *

When we get home, I say to Colleen, "Why didn't Grandma tell me my mom was twenty miles away?"

"Ask her."

"Now we know she knew."

"Ask her."

"Why didn't she tell me?"

"Will you shut up?" Colleen gives me a little push down the sidewalk. "Ask her. Then call me."

Grandma's in the kitchen. It looks like she's been doing Wii Fit Plus, because she's in loose yellow pants and a black top. Her shoes are by the door—side by side, toes aligned. Her feet are smooth and white.

She says, "Right on time," without turning around. I watch her add some turmeric to a pot of rice.

"I just saw my mother."

I get a little rush saying it like that. Fast and merciless. The spaz as assassin: that has a nice ring to it.

Her wooden spoon never stops moving. She doesn't turn around. She just says, "Did she contact you?"

I shake my head, even if she can't see me. "I found her. She lives in Azusa."

"I know, Benjamin."

I take a step forward, toward the little table where we've eaten a thousand meals. Its white napkins and spotless glasses. How many movies have I seen where things get hashed over in the kitchen? People throw things or lunge for the drawer with the knives. That won't happen here. "I know you know. Why didn't you tell me?"

She turns the fire down and goes to the cabinet for spices. Which she pretends to look for, even though they're all in alphabetical order. I know she's stalling for time. Finally she says, "Your mother wrote to me a while ago about this particular move."

"So," I say, "you knew where she was all along?"

She nods. "Periodically she'd get in touch and ask for money."

"And you'd send it?"

"Yes. It was never very much."

"Why didn't you tell me?"

"I convinced myself it was in your best interest not to know." My grandmother finally looks right at me. She examines a silver saltshaker like she's never seen it before. "At least in the beginning, it wasn't like you didn't have enough to deal with. I'd sit in the waiting room at the physical therapist's and listen to you whimper."

That stops me for a good ten seconds. "But what about when I was older? Why didn't you tell me then?"

"I didn't see the point. And I distinctly remember a conversation not long ago. You asked me if there was enough money to search for Delia, and I said, 'Do you want to do that?' And you replied, 'No, not really.'"

"But you knew where she was then."

My grandmother just nods as she stirs one of her vegetarian concoctions, then takes a tentative sip.

I tell her, "You can eat if you want to."

She either can't look at me or doesn't want to. "I've lost my appetite. Would you like some?"

"I'm not hungry, either." I turn a see-through bowl around and around. "Why did she move back down here if she doesn't want to see me?"

"I think she might."

"Did she say that?"

"Not in so many words."

"Well, I saw her first, and she looks like she's had a hard life."

"Delia was always fragile. I wasn't surprised when she finally went to pieces. In those days, I had you most of the time, anyway. If your father was out of town, she couldn't keep you overnight. The day she left, he was in Sacramento and you were wearing shoes two sizes too small. I wasn't sorry to see her go. When you were with me, I knew where you were; I knew you were safe and getting enough to eat."

I can feel — as Colleen would say — the f**king tears start way down inside me somewhere. Not in my head, where you'd think. Somewhere else. Deeper. Redder. Like my heart. "So she didn't leave because of me? Because I was just a crippled pain in the ass nobody would want?"

She shakes her head, and even her thin, rich lips quiver a little. "Is that what you think? Oh, Benjamin. She couldn't get dressed most mornings. It had nothing to do with you."

I get up and stand against the refrigerator. I let my forehead touch the big coolness. What was that story Colleen told me? That when she was little, the refrigerator would tell her she was a good girl and the sun liked her.

When I turn around, when I *can* turn around, I tell my grandma, "You haven't seen her?"

"No."

"She's pathetic. Lives in this crappy apartment and drives this old car."

"How did you get to Azusa?"

"Colleen drove. And don't start. Colleen was really nice, and Delia liked her. I could tell."

Grandma lifts the clear coffeepot and then changes her mind. But she doesn't sit down. She leans against the stove. She's not slumped, exactly. My grandmother never slumps. But she does look relaxed. Relieved, maybe. Has this secret about my mom — where she lives, how much money she wants, when she wants it — been, like, this boulder Grandma had to carry around?

"Are you angry with me?" she asks.

"I don't know."

"What do you want to do?"

"About?"

"Everything?"

I get up and stand close to her. She keeps her hands at her sides, but I hold them anyway. "I just can't believe my mother works at Target."

"And we don't know for how long. Two years ago, she moved twice in six months."

Grandma turns away and reaches into the cupboard for a cup. One of the beautiful, fragile ones she likes. The ones she never wanted me to use. For me she bought big, sturdy mugs with superheroes on them.

"Have some coffee," she says, handing me the cup, daring me to hold it steady while she pours. "You're old enough now."

So we sit there together. The light through the super-clean windows is sharp. I think of that one chair on my mother's porch. Maybe she likes sitting out there by herself, soaking up vitamin D. Maybe she's perfectly fine. Finally I say, "I guess Colleen's living with Marcie for a while."

"I know. I called Marcie not long after you left this morning. Colleen and I had breakfast together. She makes terrible choices, but she's a very bright young woman."

"You orchestrated that move?"

Grandma shrugs. "I thought it was in her best interest."

"What a cool thing to do."

"Or I'm just an old meddler who ought to stop micromanaging people's lives."

I scoot a little closer. "When I was little, I know I had C.P., but I was basically just a kid, right?"

"Of course. Maybe a little more patient than most. You'd sit for hours with your Slinky. Do you remember that?"

"Kind of."

"You liked Matchbox cars, and you had a Thomas pedal train that you just adored."

"I could do that? I didn't just pedal in a circle?"

"You managed. And you enjoyed coloring, but you weren't good at it."

"What?"

"Well, you weren't. You had this lovely coloring book about a farm, but the sheep were blue and the cows were red and the farmer and his wife were green. They looked like they'd just disembarked from a very difficult voyage."

"Where was my mom when I was busy making farmers throw up?"

"Doing her best. It was always your father or I who took you to the doctor or to the hospital for therapy. Your mother hated hospitals. On her good days, she'd get you out of bed early, take you to too many places, feed you too much ice cream, wear you out, and bring you home because you cried. On her bad days, she wouldn't come out of her bedroom."

"Didn't she need a therapist or a shrink or something?"

"I got her to see Dr. Alvarez once. She called him a quack and threw the pills out a window."

"Where's Dad in all this?"

"He seemed to make all the difference. She was at her best around him. He took her just seriously enough. He'd come home from work, tease her into getting dressed, and take her out to dinner."

"Where was I?"

"With me."

"I remember sitting on her lap. I remember that she smelled good."

"She could sing. Do you remember that? She sang for your father."

"And now she's stacking T-shirts, figuring out that the white ones go with the white ones."

Grandma stands up, takes both cups, rinses them in the sink. "I knew this day was coming, and I dreaded it. I was afraid you'd be upset with me."

"You were probably right to not tell me anything. What were you supposed to say, 'Your mom wrote and asked for another thousand dollars'?"

"She always asked about you. She always asked, "Is Benjamin all right?' "

"And that's supposed to make everything okay?"

She lets her hand land on my shoulder. "I think I'll lie down. Don't you feel like lying down?"

"A little, I guess. You go ahead."

In my room, I call Colleen, and she barely lets it ring once.

"So?"

"I'm okay. Grandma and I talked. How about you?"

"How about me what?"

"You're at Marcie's now."

"I know. It's weird. I have to work and stuff. Keep things clean. Do some dishes. Not bring any guys home, especially the syphilitic lepers I usually shoot up with."

"Give her a chance."

"Call me, like, every twenty seconds, okay? I've got the blue phantods."

"What are they?"

"Better than the screaming meemies, worse than the willies."

I know better than to nag Colleen, so A.J. and I trade a couple of e-mails, mostly about if I'm going to call Blake Edwards back and finish the interview. But I don't tell her I've seen my mother. I turn on the TV, and wouldn't you know it — on TCM there's *Mommie Dearest* with Faye Dunaway! No way, Ms. Dunaway.

* * *

Next morning when I wake up, I think about Colleen, just across the street at Marcie's. Safe and sound. IFC is going to show *Grizzly Man* in a few hours. It's a great documentary. I'll make some popcorn and Colleen and I will watch it later on.

Then my phone rings, and it's Marcie.

"Don't get upset," she says, "but Colleen is in the hospital. She didn't want to upset you, so she called me first. She's fine. Really. Little bump on the head."

I lean against my dresser. "What happened?"

"She didn't say. Just a car accident about one o'clock this morning."

"Was she loaded?"

"Why don't you come over. I'll fix us something to eat, and then we'll go to the hospital."

"Shouldn't we go now?"

"There's no point."

I take the phone away from my ear. I've been pressing way too hard. "Sure there's a point. She's all by herself."

"She's not going to know if she can come home today till the doctor makes his rounds. Probably, but they're careful about head injuries. They're just being cautious."

"So it's not just a bump on the head but a real injury?"

"Ben, she's fine. Completely coherent, completely penitent. Just come over when you get cleaned up, okay?"

A few minutes later, I'm at Marcie's front door.

"Your hair's still wet," she says. "Get in here before you catch a cold."

Marcie leads me to the nearest bathroom, throws a towel over my head, and rubs vigorously. "Let me get my hair dryer."

"I'm fine. We should go."

Marcie points to a clock. "Colleen said after ten o'clock. I'm not driving back and forth two times for nothing. I leave a deep enough carbon footprint." She puts her arm around my shoulders. "Come on. There's something I want you to see."

I follow her into the kitchen. I can see two bowls and a half gallon of milk. She points a small remote at the little flat-screen on the counter, and on comes something called *If You Can't Stand the Heat.*

"What's this?" I ask.

"I taped it the other night. It's a great little documentary about these Hispanic kids in San Antonio and their culinary arts class."

"I don't want to watch a movie. I want to see Colleen."

Marcie pulls a chair away from the table. "Will you just relax?"

"No."

"Watch this establishing shot," she says.

Anything to get this over with and get out of here. I pretend to be interested in a slow pan of a rough-looking neighborhood. Some graffiti, empty stores with FOR LEASE signs in the windows, guys on street corners, finally a high school complete with guards everywhere and metal detectors.

Then I meet the main characters—Javier, who's a soccer player; Alanna, who's got a sister in a wheelchair; and Mrs. Perez-Quiñones, called Mrs. PQ. She's the culinary arts teacher.

Marcie pushes a bowl of granola in front of me.

"I'm not hungry."

"Who said you were? Check this out—ten seconds just on Javier's muddy shoes, and all that fancy footwork on the soccer field, and then *boom!* Smash cut right to his hands dicing celery. Whoever made this knew what he was doing."

I look at the clock, pour some milk over the granola, and take a spoonful of cereal. On the screen, Javier is arguing with his girlfriend. She wants him to go somewhere with her, but he's got a job after school, and there's soccer practice, and Mrs. PQ is prepping the class for a big cook-off in Dallas.

"I can cook, baby," Javier's girlfriend says, "you don't have to. And, anyway, cooking is easy. Anybody can fry an egg."

Boom! Another smash cut.

"Not everybody can fry an egg," Mrs. PQ says. "You don't want heat more than two hundred fifty degrees. You don't want PAM; you want margarine with lecithin."

She takes a brown egg, taps the shell, carries it toward a yellow sauté pan. "Keep it a couple of inches above the skillet or grill or whatever, then let the egg just slip right out of its little shell. Oh, yeah. Cooking is sexy, okay? Don't let anybody tell you different."

Marcie grins at me, and I can't help but grin back. The close-up of the egg was perfect.

Alanna makes sure her sister gets on the bus that takes her to school, then goes back inside to study. She frowns and chews her pencil. She's got a mom, but we never see her.

Javier's mom turns up two or three times, and she says the same thing, just in different ways. "When Javie gets a scholarship for soccer, we're getting out of this neighborhood." Then she turns on the TV.

"It's all on the kid," Marcie says. "Mom just watches *telenovelas*. And the director only nails her that one time. Any more is overkill."

We eat and watch. Alanna's sister gets sick, and she almost doesn't get to go to Dallas. Javier twists an ankle and can't play soccer, but he can get around at the cook-off.

And then they win! The whole class competes, but the focus is on Javier and Alanna. Mrs. PQ hugs them both. A judge talks to Alanna, then Javier, about scholarships. Alanna calls her sister, but Javier doesn't call anybody.

"What about your mom?" asks Mrs. PQ.

"She's probably asleep in front of the TV," Javier replies.

"What about your girlfriend?"

"What about her?"

And that shot, the expression on his face as he answers his teacher, is the last frame in the film.

I sit back. "Wow."

Marcie points to the now-dark screen. "That's your future, Ben. You've got all the tools. You're smart, you're funny, and you've got a great eye. You know how photographers are always telling models how the camera loves them? Well, the camera loves you, kiddo."

I point at the clock. "It's almost ten thirty."

"Honey, Colleen's not the only girlfriend you'll ever have. You know that, don't you?"

"I guess I do."

"What'd Mrs. PQ tell her students ten times a day?"

I recite, "'If I just stay focused on my goal, it'll all pay off in the end.'"

"That's right." Marcie stands up. "So let's go. What are you waiting for?"

St. Luke's is where I used to come to do physical therapy or let somebody run another ten thousand tests. Grandma brought me even before my mother took off. It's pretty much the same, but I'm different. Thank God.

And thank Grandma and Marcie and the kids from school who were in my documentary and the company that made my camera. And Colleen.

She's in the new wing—a giant, spick-and-span igloo. Not that shape, but that white and cold. What a place—people in wheelchairs, people staggering and holding on to their IVs, people in bed with their faces turned to the wall.

When we get to her room, Marcie tells me to go on in. She'll check at the nurses' station and see what's what.

Colleen is at least sitting up and holding a *People* magazine. Her forehead is bandaged. Her tattooed arms stick out of a light-blue hospital gown.

She pretends to read until I kiss her on the cheek. She keeps her hands in her lap.

"Now you've got a girlfriend with antlers," she says.

I touch one of the bandages lightly. "A couple of bumps. They'll go away."

"Are you mad?"

I shake my head. "I'm just glad you're okay."

"Am I stupid?"

"Sometimes. Were you loaded?"

"Oh, yeah."

"Why didn't you come over? We could have just watched TV or something."

She points to a glass of water with a bendy straw, and I hand it to her. "I didn't come over because I wanted to get high. Same reason I didn't call my sponsor. And I didn't want to get ripped. I just wanted a little buzz. I don't know what that dude gave me. Creeper bud or something."

I just look at the highly polished floor.

"I didn't sleep with him, Ben. We sat in the car and smoked. When he put the moves on me, I split."

Her left foot, callused and a little dirty, is sticking out, so I pull the sheet over it.

She reaches for my hand, the sick one. "I'm driving home and thinking about your mom and then you and what a fucking sweetheart you are, and the next thing I know, I rear-end these people in a station wagon and knock myself out. They're totally okay, and my car is just, like, more dented, if that's possible, but they're worried about me and call an ambulance." She tugs at me. "I will never ever do anything like that again. Ever. I swear to God."

Just then Marcie sails in and says, "Good to go. Sign a few papers, and then they'll take you downstairs in a wheelchair. I'll get the car and meet you at the front door."

Colleen throws back the covers. "Give me a minute, Ben. I have to get dressed. Turn your back, okay?"

Across the room the closet door is open, and there are Colleen's clothes. Some I've never seen before. Flimsier. Trashier. Anti-camouflage. She wanted to be seen.

She puts both arms around me from behind, like a kidnapper. "Ben, do you love me more than anybody else in the world?"

I tell her, "You just wear me out. Do you know that?"

She holds on tighter. She says, "Don't get tired of me, okay? I don't know what I'd do if you got tired of me."

A few days later, she's got a job at the food co-op on Arroyo. I leave her messages and ask if she wants to watch a DVD or go to the Rialto, but she e-mails back and says she doesn't have time because she's studying.

> But what about your mom? I think about her
> a lot.
> Love,
> C

Love. That's new.

I can't call Delia. I don't even know if she's got a phone. I try 411, but there's no listing. So one day after school, I don't take the bus west, toward my house, but east, toward Azusa. Colleen's working, but even if she wasn't, I'd make this trip on my own.

People get off and on — people from countries the U.S. has probably invaded: a clown on his way to a kids' party, but he's wearing a headset and he snarls into it, speaking a language I've never heard before; a kid younger than me with an old-fashioned shoe-shine box, the kind with a handle and a little stand for one shoe; two brothers with plastic tyrannosauruses. They make them fight for miles, snarling and whimpering, first one winning and then the other. Three ninth-graders in do-rags swagger up and down the aisles, and we're all glad when they get off.

I have to change buses twice. I ride by places I've never been, places Grandma would never go. Every mile or so, some kids play pickup ball on bleached-out playgrounds. No matter what suburb I'm in, they look like the same kids—skinny and noisy, and at least one of them wearing a Kobe Bryant tank top. And then, just before I have to change buses again, there's a huge vacant lot with bees. Boxes of them. Colonies, I guess. Or hives. And a guy in jeans and a long-sleeved shirt and gloves and a gauzy-looking mask lifting off the lids and peering in.

Just a few blocks away from Target, my phone rings, and I answer it without checking to see who it is. I want it to be Colleen. But it's not.

"Ben? It's A.J. What's up?"

"I'm, uh . . . I'm on a bus to Azusa."

"Why?"

" 'Cause that's where my mom is."

"No way!"

"Yeah. She just . . . turned up. Recently."

"You're seeing her for the first time?"

"Second, actually."

"Wow. What's that like?"

"Confusing."

"So, have you got your camera? You should totally have your camera."

"I guess I forgot. And, anyway, my mom's kind of —"

"But, Ben. This is a real opportunity. It's a movie nobody but you can make."

"She's pretty fragile, A.J."

"Physically?"

"Yeah, but not just that. She's —"

"So in the right light, close-ups could be incredible."

"Hold on a minute. That day we met at Buster's for the first time, you said you hated those documentaries where somebody's bleeding and the guy with the camera just keeps shooting."

"Your mom's not bleeding, okay? It's totally different. Look, Ben. I've been thinking a lot lately. My parents are so successful. So is your grandma. And I want us to be successful, too. I'm not telling you to shove a camera in your mother's face. I'm just saying you could film the reunion. Did you ask her if she'd mind?"

"No, but —"

"At least ask her."

"It'd just freak her out and scare her. I don't want to be successful if I have to do stuff like that."

A few seconds go by before she says, "Conrad was right. You aren't a real filmmaker."

"Oh, well, if Conrad says so, it must be true."

"He said you were lucky to make *High School Confidential* because basically all you are is some trivia geek."

"Oh, screw Conrad."

"Some trivia geek with a slutty girlfriend."

"You don't know Colleen. Okay, she likes to dress up and shock people. Big deal."

"And sell drugs."

"Not anymore."

"And get kicked out of school for beating you up."

"You don't know the whole story. She trusted me and I let her down."

"I'm talking to you as a friend, Ben."

"Oh, great. I need a few more friends like you who'll call my girlfriend names and tell me to use my mother to make some stupid documentary nine people will see."

"I guess you're not the person I thought you were."

"Good. I don't want to be that person."

Then I hang up. I guess I was yelling a little at the end, because the people around me are staring. Well, I had a right to yell. What a stupid idea. I'll bet A.J. wouldn't interrogate her precious mother.

I go in Target through the front door this time, scan the women's section, and there she is. That same one-size-fits-nobody vest. I watch her fold and smooth. Pick up clothes people have looked at and then dropped on the floor. Find room on the rack for one more neon-colored blouse.

I make a wide half circle so Delia can see me coming. It's the opposite of hunting, where you sneak up on your prey. Pointing a camera at my mother would terrify her. It'd be like yelling at Bambi.

"Mom, it's Ben. Remember?"

She stops what she's doing and looks down into the big wheeled bin beside her. "Yes."

"Do you get a break anytime soon? I thought we'd, you know, talk or something."

"I should finish zoning this area." Her eyes light everywhere but on me.

"Please. I came on the bus. It took forever."

"Well, then. Wait for me in the snack bar. I'll sneak away."

I remember she drank 7-Up, so I buy two of those and find a semiclean table. I have weird thoughts — everybody in here, every grown-up, anyway, fell in love. At least for a little while. My parents did, and look what happened.

I think about something one of my teachers said: when somebody is really emotional, like mad or just totally excited about something, he or she speaks at the rate of 160 words a minute. My grandma does yoga and meditates and is proud of never getting — and this is her word—overwrought. I'll bet she never topped 95 words per minute in her life.

When I see my mother, I stand up. "Grandma's probably coming next time," I say.

"She drives?"

"Oh, yeah. A Cadillac."

"So that'll be easier for you." Delia picks up her gaudy cup and takes a sip. "Refreshing," she says. "Do you remember 'You Like It, It Likes You'? It was their slogan. That's why I prefer 7-Up to other soft drinks."

"It's good."

"I used to take the bus when I lived in Seattle."

"What'd you do there?" I ask.

"I worked for a little church. I answered phones and folded programs. I liked having something to do on Sundays. Sundays are hard for me."

"I don't much like Sundays. There's always school the next day."

"Are you a good student?"

I nod. "Pretty good."

"Do you play sports?"

I show her my arm. Even in long sleeves it looks wrong. "Not much."

"I like watching bowling on television. Do you watch bowling?"

"I like movies better, remember?"

She frowns and her eyes narrow. I can see her do the math. "How old are you now?"

"Sixteen."

"That much time has gone by."

I move my cup so that it touches hers. "You're not old, Mom."

"No, I guess not."

I can tell she's about to get up, so I blurt, "Look, do you need anything? You know — clothes or a better TV or something for your apartment?"

"Oh, no. I love my little cottage. I decorated it myself. I bought everything right here where I work. I get a big discount, and I know when all the sales are, and we're not supposed to do this, but we put things aside for each other. I got four big blue cups last week for a dollar!"

She looks around then like somebody might have heard. Then she sinks into the plastic chair, sliding down like a kid who doesn't want the teacher to call on her. "That man in the red vest," she whispers, "is my supervisor."

"They have to give you breaks, don't they?"

She stands up. "I should go."

"Wait." I slide just a little closer. "Do you want to come for dinner sometime?"

She thinks it over. "On a Sunday, maybe. Sundays are hard for me."

"Great."

She frowns again. "Who'll be there?"

"You and me and Grandma and maybe a neighbor from across the street and Colleen. Remember Colleen?"

She lights up for the first time. Just a little, but what a difference! "Oh, Colleen. The girl you brought out here. I liked her."

"So," I say, "pick a Sunday."

"Yes. Well, let's see. Why don't we wait and see."

"Do you have a phone?"

"Oh, yes. If someone calls in sick, I have to be available. I can work a double shift if I have to."

I hand her a clean napkin. "So, can I have the number?"

She writes, folds it in half, then quarters, and slides it across the table at me. Then she leaves. Not a handshake, for sure not a pat on the shoulder, much less a hug.

I am just so tired. I could call Grandma to come get me, but I think about what Colleen's mother always said—"You got yourself into this, so get yourself out."

I'll just wait for the bus, and, like half the people on it, I'll lean against the window and close my eyes.

COLLEEN INCHES BACK INTO MY LIFE. Not that she was totally out of it, as far as I was concerned.

I come home from school, and Colleen's there talking to Grandma. She says she's not too tired to watch a movie later. When she comes back that night after dinner, she asks if Grandma wants to watch it with us, and when I say that I don't know, she goes and asks! Then we have to wait while Grandma makes *edamame* because soybeans are better for us than popcorn.

Afterward I walk Colleen across the street, say hi to Marcie, who's up reading; then Colleen and I make out a little by the front door. It's nice. Sure, I get excited. I'm sixteen. But I don't get feverish.

We stand face-to-face, almost nose-to-nose, and she whispers, "I was checking this couple out the other day. At the store, right? At my register. And he's just staring at this little picture, so his wife is doing all the work. She's helping me bag, and before that she's got the credit card, and she unloaded the cart, and I'm thinking, *What a dick. Look at your stupid little picture somewhere else.* And then he shows her, and she smiles this huge smile and shows me, and it's an ultrasound. She's pregnant. They're both so happy. He was, like, mesmerized. And there I am, judging him."

"You didn't know."

"Maybe it's all these people I'm calling. All the amends I'm making. I felt like I should apologize to that couple."

"Don't be so hard on yourself."

"I guess. Did you just brush your teeth? You taste like fucking candy."

"Actually, I did. When I went to the bathroom after dinner. I thought if you wanted to kiss me, I'd be ready."

All of a sudden she holds me so tight. Seizes me. Grips me. "I fucking do not deserve you."

I smooth her short hair. "Yeah, you do. You deserve better than me."

"Really? Like who?"

"I didn't mean anybody in particular."

"Like Brad Pitt? I would do Brad Pitt in a heartbeat."

"There goes that Hallmark moment."

She laughs and asks, "So, what about the elusive Delia?"

I shrug. "I call and she doesn't pick up. Is she not there, or is she screening her calls? I was all gee-I-found-my-mom-again for a few days. Now I'm kind of mad. I think if you don't want to see me, say so. I'll be fine. I've seen you, and you're nothing to write home about."

Colleen shakes her head. "Don't be that way. We have to go out there again. I've got Tuesday off. Can you go Tuesday after English?"

I like school. Before Colleen, school and movies were all I did. Now I still like it. Maybe even more. People talk to me, they ask me what's playing at the mall and if anything is worth seeing. They're stuck on a math problem or an *être* verb involving movement. I don't always know, so we figure it out together. They ask about Colleen and actually seem sincere.

The last class of the day is English. I walk in to find this substitute teacher right out of Central Casting — ponytail, cords, sandals — writing on the board:

the goldfish held the cats hostage

He asks, "Keeping in mind the whole poem in your text, but concentrating on just this one line, what do you think the poet is trying to say?"

He's the opposite of Ben Stein in *Ferris Bueller's Day Off,* but he sounds just like him. "Anybody?" he asks. "Anybody?"

Oliver Atkins looks at me, then falls facedown on his desk in a pretend faint. Three or four girls giggle. They're too pretty for poetry, anyway. Boots are all the rage, and they have theirs out in the aisles, where everybody can see who has the shiniest, the highest heeled, the most expensive.

The sub moves a plastic bag of baby carrots to one side and consults his seating chart. He hasn't shaved, and I wonder if the office called him at 7:05 this morning and he shot out of bed. Under that Gap shirt, I'll bet he's got a pale, bony chest like John Keats.

He asks, "Mr. Atkins?"

Oliver looks up, bright-eyed, then gets to his feet. "Yes, sir?"

"You don't have to stand up."

"But we always stand, sir. As a gesture of respect."

That's a lie, but everybody likes it.

"Whatever," says the sub. (I know he has a name, and I know he wrote it on the board, but I can't remember it.) Right now he looks like he's heartily sorry he's a vegetarian and what he really wants is a burger and a whip. "What do you think the poet is getting at?"

"I'm not sure," Oliver says, "that he's getting at anything. Our regular teacher says that poems should be, not mean." He points. "That line on the board is interesting, though. It turns the usual power structure on its head. The slaves turn on the plantation owner, the UPS man on the Amazon-addicted customer, the abused on the abuser, the students on their teacher."

Now the sub looks up like this unexpected turbulence will cause the oxygen mask to drop down. He tells us to talk among ourselves. He puts another poem on the board. Finally, the bell rings and he collapses into the chair.

Oliver grins at me. On the way out, the jocks who regularly torment Oliver and call him *faggot* cuff him around harmlessly. Attaboy. The done unto becomes the doer.

As I pass the teacher, he looks at his watch, which is a

Little Mermaid model, the one where she's wearing the blue bra top and her hair is bougainvillea red.

When I see that watch, I wonder if he isn't an interesting guy, after all. His girlfriend gave him that. Or his kid. Or, even better, he bought it for himself.

So there's a possible documentary: *The Secret World of Substitute Teachers*. Maybe I wouldn't be exploiting anybody if I talked to them. Maybe they want their story told.

I tell him, "See you tomorrow, maybe."

He looks up and offers me one of the tiny carrots from his stash. "Yeah, maybe. I hope so. I could use the money."

"You don't know ahead of time? They just call you?"

"There are long-term gigs. Some old guy dies or something. But usually I just wait by the phone like a pudgy virgin with acne."

That makes me laugh, and that makes him grimace.

"Sorry," he says, "that wasn't very PC of me."

"That's cool. I'm not very PC myself." I take a step toward the door. "See you."

"Yeah. Tomorrow, I hope. Thanks, man."

Thanks, man. What is he — ten years older than me? Eight? A few months ago — Before Colleen — I was the pudgy virgin with acne waiting by the phone. Well, not pudgy. I never had acne, and the phone was a DVD. But the virgin part for sure.

* * *

174

When Colleen pulls up, I tumble into the car.

"Lean over here and kiss me passionately," she says. "It'll ramp your street cred to new heights."

I do, and she puts her heart into it. Then zips away from the red zone. A couple of kids I know from English glance up and nod in that I'm-too-cool-to-wave way, but I know they saw.

We pass a huge McDonald's on the corner just a block from the on-ramp to the 210. I like the primary colors. Kids wiping their hands on their good clothes. Kids in what look like pajamas, but it's almost four. One little boy trying to push his backpack up the longest slide, like a kiddie version of Sisyphus. I point and Colleen gets it. Then she laughs when the kid almost makes the top, reaches for a handhold, just misses, and slides all the way back down.

She's in pants with extra loops and side pockets, a black sweater, and blue Vans. I wonder if Marcie took her shopping.

Colleen likes to weave in and out of traffic, make all the lights, then zoom onto the freeway. We're zipping along just past the speed limit — and most things are just past the speed limit with her — when she says, "I heard from Ed. He's so crazy to see me, he's going AWOL. And then we'll probably go on a little crime spree — rob banks, jack a few cars."

"Keep books out of the library way past their due dates."

"Me and Ed forever. That's about your worst fear, isn't it?"

"That and big dogs charging at me."

"You'd be fine without me. You and that icy bitch A.J."

"A.J.'s history. She got all mad because I wouldn't shove a camera in my mother's face and make her cry."

"What'd I just say? Another cold-blooded opportunist."

"She's way more hard-core than I thought."

"I guess you know she doesn't wear underpants."

"It's the first thing she told me. That and where the gold in her backyard is buried."

"You jest, but it's true. Have you seen those low-rise jeans of hers? No panty line."

"I'll take your word for it."

"Where is your little camera, anyway? You used to point that thing at me twenty-four seven."

"I'm giving it a rest. I'm not sure I want to make any more documentaries. They're kind of nosy."

"That's why they're interesting. You should meet these aliens who work at the co-op with me. This one guy is obsessed with Ping-Pong. It's all he talks about: backhand slams, punch serves, you name it."

"Have you seen him play?"

"On his iPod, yeah. He's got, like, matches of the century on there. Featuring him."

"And he's good?"

"Scary good."

"What's his name?"

"Walter, but he wants me to call him the Demolisher."

"Christopher Walken was already in a movie about Ping-Pong: *Balls of Fury*."

"That was stupid. You'd never make anything stupid. That thing you did about those kids at school? That was really tasty. And if you meet the Ping-Pong guy and don't like him, how about some alcoholic sisters who work produce? They play Monopoly twelve hours a day."

"If there's anything that'll keep an audience riveted, it's seeing a top hat hop around a board."

"Except these girls are crazy. They play this really caffeinated version, so one of them wins about every half hour. Three or four wins makes one of them an angel. Three or four more and she's an archangel. A few more and she's Super Queen of Heaven. It's not about Monopoly or table tennis. It's about obsession, right?"

I sit up straighter. "And they're grown-ups. They'd know what they were getting into."

"They're grown-up fruitcakes, and they're dying for attention."

"You might be onto something."

She looks over at me. "So, I'm the one, aren't I?"

"With grammar like that, who could resist."

She pretends to scowl. "You know what, Tiny Tim? What say we find a little park and play a little catch? Maybe do some wind sprints."

I take her right hand off the wheel, kiss it, and let it rest on my semi-useless leg. She leaves it there, too, the rest of the way to Azusa.

A person can get used to anything. I got used to limping all the time. I got used to being alone. All I really mean, I guess, is that I'm used to Target. Used to my mother being there, bending over to pick up a dress that somebody in flip-flops tossed on the floor.

Except she's not in her section.

"What now?" I ask Colleen.

"Give it a minute. She could be in the bathroom."

One of the racks looks junky, with dresses crammed against each other, so I straighten those out a little.

"Did you ever buy stuff from Target?" I ask.

Colleen shakes her head. "I was raised by wolves." She reaches for my hand. "C'mon, let's check the dining room, with its chandeliers and liveried footmen."

Sure enough, my mother is in the snack bar, sipping at her favorite soft drink. The one she likes and that likes her back.

"Mom," I say. "It's me. Ben. And Colleen."

"Oh, dear. Where did you come from?"

I point. "Okay if we sit down?"

She nods. She has deep, dark half circles under both eyes.

"We're not going to keep you," Colleen says, "but we just wanted to check — you're still good for dinner sometime soon, right?"

She leans back in the plastic chair. "I know what I said, but I'm just so tired."

Colleen reaches for my mother's hand and holds it. "Man, tell me about it. I've got the register to worry about; I work the loading dock; I stock shelves. My back hurts; my legs are sore. And it's like that from three in the afternoon to ten o'clock at night."

"Oh," my mother says. "That's a terrible shift. I've worked it, but I don't like it." She looks at me then. "You don't understand, Ben. You can't."

I start to protest. Colleen cuts me off.

"Forget about him. He's a freaking brainiac." She points to her forehead. "It's all up here with him. A's all the time, honor society, the whole nine yards."

"You're that bright?" she asks.

Colleen answers for me. "Bright? Are you kidding? You need sunglasses just to be around him. But he doesn't work, Delia. He's not like us."

Her other hand covers Colleen's. "It's hard, isn't it?"

"You can say that again." She nods my way. "You know what this one does? Makes movies. Sits on his butt in his little canvas chair with his name on it and says, 'Roll 'em!'

How hard can that be? I mean, he's talented, and, okay, he shows in Hollywood and places like that, but he doesn't get his hands dirty like we do."

Delia looks at me. "You're in Hollywood?"

"At a gallery," I say. "No big deal."

"Hollywood." My mother says the three magic syllables.

"When you come to dinner," Colleen says, "you can see his latest. Okay?"

Delia takes a deep breath. "I don't know. I'm exhausted all the time."

I tell her, "We'll come get you. You won't have to drive."

"I can drive, Benjamin. I'm a perfectly good driver. I drove from Seattle, Washington."

"I didn't say you weren't a good driver. I just meant—"

Colleen leans toward my mother and half whispers, "Let's go to the bathroom."

"What?" she asks.

"I want to go to the bathroom. Come with me. Girls always go to the bathroom together."

That seems to light my mother up a little. "All right." And she gets to her feet.

Colleen peers down at me. "You stay here, and if the handsome waiter comes, order for me, okay? I'll have the escargot."

I watch them walk away, Colleen's arm linked in my mother's. Colleen's tall and thin as a reed; my mom's a little thick and stooped over. She's looking up at Colleen and nodding. That's a picture I'd like to have in a frame.

I listen to the hubbub around me, mostly kids begging for more of everything. A couple of guys who work there sit across from each other with tub-size drinks, both of them plugged into separate iPods. Maybe that's why they work — to buy stuff like that. They probably live at home.

Those people from the food co-op Colleen told me about sound interesting. They actually do stuff. *High School Confidential* was just talking heads. The editing made it as good as it was, and Marcie helped me with that.

A few minutes later, Colleen comes back by herself. I ask, "Where's my mom?"

Colleen points. "Waiting for us in the men's section."

"What's she doing — ?"

"She's really sorry about what happened twelve years ago. She's kind of ashamed of herself and hopes that you'll just forgive her and be patient with her."

"She actually said that?"

Colleen squirms a little. "Not in so many words."

"What exact words did she say?"

"Um, that there are some sale items you might be interested in. But you just have to read between the lines."

"And that's what you were doing in the bathroom? Reading between the lines?"

"She loves you, Ben. She's just . . . I don't know. Shell-shocked or something." Colleen tugs at me. "Now, c'mon. She wants to buy you a T-shirt. It's important to her."

"Is she ever coming to dinner?"

"Next week. If she can."

"BENJAMIN?"

"I'm ready, Grandma."

"It's seven."

"We're just going across the street."

Grandma has always been super-prompt, and while I'm on my way to the door, where she's waiting, I won-der if it's because she took me to so many appointments when I was little. Endless doctors' appointments and physical therapy appointments. What in the world would I have done without her?

She's holding the door open, but I let her go first. When I'm right beside her, I put my arm through hers.

"I'm perfectly steady on my feet, Benjamin."

"It's not that. I just like you."

"Well, of all the things to say."

But she doesn't pull away.

It's dusk or evening or not-quite-night or one of those. It's usually really clear in Los Angeles. But it's hazy tonight, and that reflects headlights and streetlights and millions of TVs.

I know the stars are up there, though. Right now we're studying constellations. In English, no less. We have to memorize a whole list of them — not just the marquee ones, like the Big Dipper or Orion, but Canis Major and Boötes the Herdsman, too. And then we write about them.

They've all got stories. Myths about how they got to be who they are and where they are. Some of the kids in my class are really creative. They make up new constellations like Redbrick Silo or Korean Grocer, then tell how they got their names. Which gods they cheesed off or, maybe, were kind to when they came down here in disguise, which is what the gods like to do.

We'll make a little constellation tonight — Colleen and me, Marcie and Grandma and my mother. A constellation that's too unstable to have a name yet. I don't ring Marcie's doorbell with trepidation, exactly, but I do wonder how this evening is going to play out.

Grandma whispers, "I enjoy seeing Colleen working in the yard."

"She's clerking at that natural-foods market on Arroyo."

"I never thought I'd say this, but you make an interesting couple."

"Wow, I never thought you'd say that, either."

Almost every night now, Colleen and I watch a movie together. Except she's in her room at Marcie's and I'm in my room across the street. Sometimes we don't say ten words for an hour and a half. But we know the other person is there. I hear a little *clink* when her glass touches a saucer. I hear the toilet flush and then the rustle of covers when she settles down in bed again. Every now and then she'll say, "Ben?" and I say, "I'm right here." In a weird way it's more — and I guess the word I want is *intimate* — it's more intimate than anything Colleen and I do. And I mean anything.

Just then Colleen opens the door. She's in a tangerine-colored crewneck, blue pants (but not jeans), and old Doc Martens with the laces undone.

I tell her, "No mother yet."

"Give her time." She looks me up and down. "You are too cute in that shirt."

But Colleen keeps the PDAs to a minimum around my grandmother, and maybe that explains the long-sleeved sweater: if there's a tattoo in the forest and nobody sees it, is it really there?

"C'mon in, you guys," she says.

There's a drop cloth crumpled up at the foot of one wall, some spackle, and two or three cans of paint. One of the first things Marcie told me when we got to be friends was that she was almost always discontented. I remember we were talking about the camera she was going to loan me so I could make *High School Confidential,* and she just said it. How restless she was. I liked her right away.

Marcie comes charging out of the kitchen. Big smile. Arms open. She likes to wear caftans, and tonight's is green with a bamboo print. She hugs everybody. Even Colleen, who she saw about two minutes ago. Marcie is just that way.

"Sit down," she says.

I hold Grandma's chair like a good boy. Colleen watches and then says, "Unfuckingbelievable."

"No one ever did that for you?" Grandma asks.

"Get serious. My mother threw a chair at me once."

I'm around the table before Colleen can say anything else. I pull the chair out a little and wait. Colleen just stares at it, then sits down carefully.

"So weird," she says.

Marcie arrives then, putting a big wooden bowl in the middle of the table. Marcie's a good cook. I can see avocado and tomato, two kinds of lettuce, and arugula. And candied walnuts on the side.

"Mrs. B.," Marcie says, "I've got some chardonnay."

"If you're having some."

Marcie shakes her head. "I've been going to AA again."

That makes me look up from coveting all the walnuts.

She says, "I convinced myself I could have a drink or two. A spritzer after I've been working in the garden. A nice cabernet with dinner. Then two or three days ago, I'm at the store and I pick up a bottle of gin. I love gin. A couple of martinis, and there they are again — songs from the underworld."

Colleen says, "You're doing good."

Her hand lands on Colleen's tufty hair like a blessing. "And so are you." Then she turns away. "Be right back with the entrée."

Grandma asks, "So you two struggle together?"

"Oh, yeah," Colleen answers. "When I say she's doing good, I just mean that it's after seven but she's not drunk and I'm not loaded."

Grandma looks around. "And how does your mother feel about this arrangement?"

"She knows I'm somewhere with a roof over my head, but I'd never tell her where. Marcie's got nice stuff, and I don't want somebody coming in and cleaning her out."

"Someone your mother knows would do that?"

"When I was little, she'd come home from work, take a bottle of wine into the bathroom, and sit in the tub with bubbles up to her chin. She'd put a razor blade on the edge of the bathtub, and she'd call me in and say, 'If I used this, you wouldn't know what to do, would you?'

At first it made me cry, and I'd beg her not to kill herself. And then, when I was about twelve, one night I yelled at her and told her to go ahead and do it. I was sick of her, anyway, and I'd be okay on my own. Then I went and stayed with one of my girlfriends from school."

"She didn't ask where you were?"

"Now or then?"

"Either."

Colleen shakes her head. "My mom's kind of crazy, but different from Ben's mom, who's just out of it. Delia's like somebody who's been in a car wreck; my mom is like the person who hit her and then drove off like it didn't happen." Then she stands up. "Sit tight. I'm going to go help Marcie."

Grandma waits till the door swings shut behind Colleen before she says, "I've never heard anyone talk so blithely about such tragic circumstances." She takes a small bite of salad, then says, "Except doctors, maybe. I've been at fund-raisers where physicians come back from Ghana or Peru and tell the most horrible stories in such a matter-of-fact tone."

Colleen walks in with a roasted chicken on a platter. She waits while I move the salad bowl and a few other things. She takes a huge knife and an oversize fork and goes to work carving.

"Where'd you learn to do that?" I ask.

"The butcher at work likes me. He's tall and

handsome, goes to the gym, works with Greenpeace in the summer, and rescued this baby seal that he's taught to talk. But don't be jealous, Ben. You've got a better camera."

Colleen's a real chatterbox tonight, and I wonder if that means anything about her equilibrium. I hope not. It's probably just a lot of Pepsi, anyway. A little of anything is never enough for Colleen.

"We're not going to wait for my mom?" I ask. "This dinner's kind of for her."

"She said not to," Colleen informs us.

"You talked to her?"

"Sure. I gave her my number when you and I were out there last week."

"How come she talks to you and not to me?"

"She doesn't know what to say to you," my grandma says.

I just look at her.

Colleen nods. "That's right."

Marcie holds out her plate for a drumstick but looks at me as she says, "Let's talk about something else for a minute. I've been prowling the Net for you, Ben. There's a ten-day film workshop this summer in Aspen. You should go." She looks at my grandmother. "He should go, Esther."

Esther. I know that's my grandmother's name, but I almost never hear anybody use it. Marcie usually calls her Mrs. B. And to everybody else she's Mrs. Bancroft. Colleen calls her Granny, but not to her face.

"Didn't we see an Esther in one of those old movies you make me watch?" Colleen asks. "Always in a swim-suit."

"Sure, Esther Williams. *Bathing Beauty.* Almost out-grossed *Gone with the Wind.*"

Grandma straightens her shoulders. "My girlfriends thought I was just as pretty as Esther Williams, and I could swim, too."

"Get out of town," Colleen says.

"Why is that so unbelievable?" Grandma stands up and puts her napkin on the chair. Where it belongs. "I'll be back in a moment."

And out the door she goes.

"Is she mad?" Colleen asks.

"She doesn't sound mad."

I look at Marcie, who just shakes her head and says, "I always figured she was born in cashmere separates and only got out of them to bathe."

"Well, while we're alone," I say, "how much is that summer thing you were talking about?"

"Who cares? Your grandmother can afford it, and it's got everything—three films in three weeks, sixteen millimeter or three-chip DV, continuity work, composi-tion, blocking, you name it."

"You should go," Colleen says. "Don't worry about

me while you're off with beautiful, talented girls who share your passion for filmmaking. I'll just work my minimum-wage job and help the butcher beat his meat."

"Hey, I'll go to film school if you'll go to comedy school. Work on your timing. Get some new material."

Colleen comes around the table, leans into me, kisses me on the neck, licks my ear. She's just kidding around, but it still makes my heart beat fast. Partly because it turns me on, but partly because I used to see girls at school do that to their boyfriends, and I thought it'd never happen to me in a million years.

Marcie leans back in her chair. "I was born in this stupid little town with one stoplight and one cop. Whenever he caught high-school kids parked somewhere and making out, all he'd ever say was, 'Take that somewhere else.'"

"Did you go to high school there?" Colleen asks.

Marcie nods. "They'd bus kids in from the boonies. There were maybe forty in my graduating class. Mostly girls. The boys dropped out and went to work or enlisted. We had a girls' track team, though. Not that anybody cared. We just ran because we liked it. There weren't any parents or boyfriends. Two of the girls were gay but didn't know it, so we more or less protected them."

"But you knew."

"Nobody ever said anything."

Colleen asks, "Who did you protect them from?"

Marcie shrugs. "They were just really happy when we were all in our stupid, baggy gym suits. Then they got married after graduation and were miserable."

"Not to each other."

"In Oklahoma? Are you kidding?"

Colleen looks at the door like this conversation will end when Grandma comes back, and she doesn't want it to.

"But you got out," she says.

"Oh, yeah. As soon as I could. I wanted to experience life."

"Like?" Colleen's eyes are bright and hot.

"Oh, like I had this boyfriend my first year in college. I knew he was coming over, just not when, exactly. So I'd read until he showed up, but I'd be nervous. 'All het up,' as my mother used to say. Then I'd hear his car, and I'd put a piece of paper in the book and put it back on the shelf. By that time I'd be on my feet."

"Were you naked?" Colleen asks.

"Gee, no. He thought I was a nice girl. And, anyway, he liked to tear my clothes off. I didn't have a lot of money, so I'd buy shirts and blouses from the Goodwill and sometimes just sew the buttons back on."

"What happened to him?"

"Oh, he was married. My heart was broken."

I ask, "Did you finish the books?"

Marcie shakes her head. "I still don't know what happens at the end of *The Great Gatsby*."

Colleen takes a bite of chicken before she says, "Well, I'm not telling my stories. They're too sordid."

"And you're my story," I say, "so we all know that one."

We just sit for a while. Water from one of the little fountains gurgles and drips. The candles flicker, lean hard to the left for a couple of seconds, then straighten up. We grin at each other like something slightly magical just happened.

I think how much I like this: sitting at a table with my friends. Or one friend and my girlfriend and my grandma. Or maybe it's really my girlfriend and two friends, because ever since the secrets about my mom came out, it's like Grandma can relax. What would it be like with my mother here? Just thinking about it makes me nervous.

When the front door opens again, I stand up, because that's what I was taught to do when "a lady" enters the room. Grandma's carrying a blue plastic bin. I point to the nearest chair, but she says, "No. This will be fine."

She means one of the tall stools that I've sat on and talked to Marcie while she cooked. But it's a few yards away from the table, and Grandma has her back to us as she takes off the white lid. What's in there that she might not want us to see? It's not like her to just be dramatic.

She turns around, holding pictures. Photographs, maybe, is what she would say. All in frames — silver, gold, ebony. I just know she was careful to have the frames complement the snaps. Or she paid someone to do it.

"Here we are," she says, propping one of them on the table.

"Oh, my God," says Colleen. "Look at you."

My grandmother in a bathing suit that's almost psychedelic: swirls of purple, white, orange, black.

"Elastic waffle nylon with tummy-control panels and a floral Hawaiian print." She recites the specs wistfully. It has that long-ago-and-far-away tone. One I'm not used to from her. When I was little and she read to me, Red Riding Hood would speed through the forest like a little fire engine.

"What's that ruffly thing on your head?" asks Colleen.

"It's a bathing cap with a rather ornate —"

Colleen asks me, "Didn't something like that fall on Sigourney Weaver in deep space and try to suck out her brain?"

Marcie looks at my grandmother and says, "You look wonderful."

"I went to the country club every day," Grandma says.

"You could swim in that getup?"

"I swam the sidestroke to keep my makeup dry. I wore a lipstick by Elizabeth Arden called Perfect Red." She looks at me. "Your grandfather loved that shade. He once had me kiss him on the neck so a little showed up on his white dress shirt. Then he went to work. He wanted people to kid him."

"Holy shit," Colleen says. But reverently. I know what she means. I've never heard Grandma talk like this.

She says, "I was pregnant when this photograph was taken. I just didn't know it."

She walks to the bin, moves a few things, comes back. "Here's your father when he was three."

He's a solemn-looking little kid in short pants and a striped sweater. A black-and-white dog lies at his feet.

"What's the dog's name?" I ask.

"Owen." Then she pairs it up with another one. "And then here you are, Ben."

"You guys look alike," says Colleen. "Except both his legs are the same size."

I ask, "Where's Mom?"

Grandma looks at Marcie, then me. She retreats to the bin, returns with half a dozen pictures, which she lays out slowly, like tarot cards: Mom and Dad, him with his arm around her; he's grinning. Mom and Dad and me at Disneyland; he's holding me. Dad and me beside his car, a cool-looking convertible. Me in the backyard with a fat plastic bat and him pretending to pitch a beach ball. Me on a tricycle and Dad making sure I don't tip over. Mom by herself, shading her eyes with one hand and looking out of the frame. At Seattle, maybe.

"There's a lot of just my dad and me," I say.

"Your mother preferred lying down with a cold washcloth on her forehead," Grandma says.

Just then Colleen's phone rings. The timing is too perfect. I sigh and sit back in my chair. Grandma's hand floats through the space between us and lands on my shoulder. We listen to one side of the conversation.

"It's all right, Delia," Colleen says. "If you have to go in, you have to go in. Yes. Yes, absolutely another time. Ben and I'll come out next week. Sure."

"I knew it." I look at Grandma. "Didn't you know it?'

She admits, "I certainly wondered if she'd be able."

I hit the table with my fist. Not hard, just decisively. "Every time it's like starting over with her. I drive twenty miles or take a stupid bus, and it's just a rerun of the last time. Why do I even bother?"

"She said she wants us to come to her house," Colleen says. "That's progress."

"Well, great. Maybe we can all sit in that one chair."

"You don't have to do any more than you already have if you don't want to," Marcie says. "We all really are on our own paths, Ben, and it's just possible that yours and your mother's don't actually intersect."

Colleen puts down her fork. "That's such bullshit.

Ben has to try. Delia's his mom." She looks at Marcie. "How can you say fucking heartless shit like that?"

Marcie takes a sip of Perrier and says evenly, "I'm just presenting alternatives."

"Well, that one stinks."

I say, "I know what Marcie means. Maybe my mom just wants to be left alone. She sure acts like it sometimes."

Grandma shakes her head. "No, I agree with Colleen. You have to try."

Then we don't talk about that anymore. We eat and don't look at each other. Little by little, we start again—Colleen's job at the co-op, movies that the Academy drones overlooked at Oscar time, what's going on at my school and Colleen's, and Colleen herself, who is embarrassed to be getting good grades. She adds, "Class participation is a lot easier when you're not unconscious."

Everybody listens, even the ones propped up in their expensive frames—my dad puts down the beach ball, Delia turns around and smiles, Grandma takes off that amazing swim cap and runs one hand through her short hair.

"Ben and I will clean up," Colleen says when we've finished.

"It's your job," Marcie reminds her, with just a little chill in her voice.

Colleen calmly picks up the four bowls. "You want to wash or dry, Ben?"

When we're alone in the kitchen, I ask her, "What was that about?"

"That's just Marcie being Marcie." Colleen turns off the hot water and picks up a pair of blue rubber gloves. "I loved seeing those pictures. And I'll bet Granny brought them over for Delia to see, too."

"I'm not going to give up on her."

"I know, baby. You might be a wormy little spaz who's spent way too much time indoors, but you're not a quitter."

Then she kisses me.

Colleen washes and I dry. Once, we hear Marcie and Grandma laughing in the other room, and we look at each other and make that you-never-know face.

When I reach for a saucer that Colleen is holding out, I tell her, "I've seen this kitchen scene in about nine thousand movies."

"Usually the guy's traded his cojones for a cardigan sweater, right? Who was that *Father Knows Best* dude, anyway?"

"Robert Young. But that was television. Played the most well-adjusted guy in the world, but in his real life he tried to commit suicide."

"No shit?" Colleen freezes. White suds on the blue glove. A dripping dish halfway to the rinse water. The sleeve of her tangerine sweater pushed way up, and there's that tattooed race car, complete with wavy speed lines zooming toward her shoulder.

"It's cool that you know that stuff," she says. "It puts things in perspective. You know what I wonder? How many people watch movies and shit and then want to be like what they see. They don't think about some actor taking off his, like, costume and turning into somebody who needs to stop at the market on the way home."

I say, "There're probably a hundred seminars a year with people trying to figure out if watching movies is bad for kids or not. The same experts over and over. They probably all travel on the same bus. And nobody knows for sure. I watched who-knows-how-many movies. I was a spaz when I started and a spaz ten years later. Movies didn't change me; you did."

She leans into a greasy platter. "Just for the record — after a night like this, I want to smoke a blunt about as big as King Kong's thumb."

"Was it that bad? You seemed totally —"

"I was fucking nervous. What if Delia canceled? How were you going to feel about that? What would you do if she did? So I wanted to get high."

I pull her toward me. She resists, and then she doesn't.

"But I'd kind of hate myself afterward," she says. "And you'd hate me."

"I'd never hate you."

She turns around, drapes both arms across my

shoulders, and asks, "Why are you so fuckin' nice to me? I'm really not a nice person."

"Remember when we were in Target that first time? And you went over to my mom and told her that her son was standing by the polyester separates? And then you ate that stupid lunch in that stupid snack bar and you were so patient and sweet to her?"

Colleen nods. "Well, okay. Maybe I am pretty lovable sometimes."

"And modest, too."

There's that smirk of hers, the one I like so much. She tightens her grip on me. She makes sure I can feel her from my forehead to my knees. She gets right up next to my ear and hisses, "Leave your window open tonight."

"Why?" I gasp. "When Grandma goes to bed, I'll just unlock the front door."

She shakes her head. "I want to come in the window. That's how Dracula does it."

A couple of nights later, here's what I'm staring at:

> Find the constant k such that the system of the two equations $2x + ky$ and $5x - 3y$ has no solutions.

I literally say "Huh?' out loud, and just then the phone rings.

"Remember Crystal and Amber," Colleen asks, "those

dancers we ran into at Buster's? Well, they've got a new place, and they're having a party tonight. Right now. They want us to drop by."

I close my math book. "Are you crazy? They're druggies."

"Just Crystal. Amber's totally vegan and thinks her body is a fucking temple. We'll be there for, like, two minutes. Just enough time for me to drop off some guacamole. C'mon, Ben. I don't want to go alone."

"This is a bad idea, Colleen."

"Excellent. I'll be right over. Wear that sweater I like."

Crystal and Amber's new place is in a brand-new building about half a block from one of the light-rail stations. A banner announces, ONLY 8 LEFT!

The ground floor isn't residential, though. All that's upstairs. But there aren't any street-level businesses yet, just big, empty spaces and FOR LEASE signs.

Colleen parks against the building, and I follow her up a curved ramp like we're the most unlikely pair of animals boarding the ark. Everything is brand-new. I can smell the paint.

Colleen's in a Bebe T-shirt cropped and ripped in all the right places, very short skirt, and precarious-looking shoes.

I ask, "Aren't you cold?"

"It's a party, right? These are my party clothes." She

leans in and kisses me. "Stop worrying. I just dress like a drug-addicted slut. I'm clean and sober, and I'm going to stay clean and sober."

I tell her, "This is not a good idea."

"So wait in the car. You're not Lassie. You don't have to go everywhere with me. I'm not going to fall in a well."

"Take it easy. Since when do you know so much about Lassie?"

"In rehab they had all these warm and fuzzy DVDs. The whole Lassie platinum set: *Lassie Come Home, Lassie Saves the School, Lassie Gets a PhD.*"

Just then two girls come up the stairs and pass us, their heels clicking. "Hey, Colleen," one of them says.

"Yeah, hi." But she doesn't turn around. She leans into me. "Baby, just ten minutes. Amber's my friend, okay? I don't want to just blow her off."

I tell her, "Listen — if I was addicted to movies and they'd almost ruined my life, I wouldn't be able to go to the mall, because there'd be a multiplex and I'd be tempted."

She takes my face in both hands. "Movies have already ruined your life. Look what you've got for a girlfriend."

Colleen has three or four ways of kissing me. This one is absolutely my drug of choice.

"All right," I manage to say. "Just ten minutes."

Then she barges in without knocking. Everybody looks up — a white kid in size 78 jeans; Amber and

Crystal, in tank tops and low-slung pants; an older guy in velour sweats and what used to be called bling; a girl in a long, pretend-leather coat and big, clunky shoes; a blonde wearing earmuff-size headphones, dancing by herself in the corner; and Mr. Cool: hair slicked back like Michael Douglas in *Wall Street,* aviator shades, leather sport coat.

Ugly brown furniture with cigarette burns, but huge TVs — a giant plasma on the wall with ESPN on mute, and a smaller flat-screen sitting right beside its box, which hasn't been opened so much as torn apart by something with rabies.

Colleen hugs Crystal like she hasn't seen her in years. Then I get introduced: Mr. Velour is Randy, the ghetto-poseur is Jax ("with an *x*"), faux-leather coat is Dee, and Mr. Cool is Arthur.

Randy — who's got a phone plastered to one ear — asks Colleen, "Who's this guy again?"

"From school."

"He looks like a narc."

"Relax, Randy. Jesus." She tugs at me. "Let's take the tour."

I stop a couple of yards away and say, "'He looks like a narc'? We're getting out of here."

"I just want to tell Amber I saw the whole place and I love her new shower curtain with the fish on it."

We go down a short hall, through a door with just a hole where the knob should be.

There are two dressers, three posters taped to the walls (half-naked girls wearing not much and holding foaming glasses of brew), and two beds. Neither one is exactly made, but one has a girl in it. She's covered up with what looks like an electric blanket. I can see the naked prongs at one end. It's not plugged into anything.

Colleen leans over her. "Hey, Luci. You okay?"

She's groggy and has trouble focusing. "Leave me alone, okay? I'm behind a bunch of Valium. Randy gave me a tab of something weird. I just want to sleep."

Colleen leads me into the hall, where she whispers, "Fuck."

I ask, "Is she okay?"

"No, she's not okay. I have to find Amber."

I wander over to a card table loaded down with white bread, lunch meat, pale tomato slices, and a mustard jar with crust around the top. Jax cruises up, makes a huge sandwich, plops that on a paper plate decorated with clowns, then adds two brownies.

"Not hungry?" he asks.

"Listen, do you know that girl in the bedroom?"

"Luci? Oh, yeah. Luci knows what she's doing. C'mon, let's sit."

We settle in front of the little TV. Arthur lounges right underneath the giant plasma, and Crystal brings him things. They must communicate by telepathy, because he never says a word. Compared to Randy, who shouts,

"Unbelievable. You call me and tell me that? Me? Do you know who I am?"

Jax lowers his voice. His mustardy breath wafts over me.

"Remember when you were in high school and the cute guys got all the prime trim? Now it's the heavy hitters with the designer pain relief. Take you, okay— you're crippled and all, but if you were to, like, go into any club with, say, a zip of train wreck, those girls would be all over you. Those pole dancers, man, they can smell primo product from across the room. Like, Randy never has to be alone unless he wants to be. He's got this grow house out in the boonies with tunnels and underground lights and guards from Thailand who are, like, blind but deadly with their hands or five-sided throwing stars. And he knows this lab in Mexico where some MIT genius Frankensteins some amazing shit. I smoked some once, and I'm, like, saving to go down there. Forget margaritas and señoritas." He finally takes a breath, then leans closer. "But the thing is with Randy—don't ever piss him off to the extent that he says he's going to his car. He ever says he's going to his car, get your ass out the back, because he's supposed to have an AK in there."

Just then Colleen comes and leans over the couch. "Sit tight, Ben. We're not going anywhere until I'm sure Luci is okay."

Jax watches her walk away. "Man, she could totally

dance at the club if she wanted to. What a bangin' bod she's got."

"I'll tell her you said so. She might want to put that on her college application."

"Wow, I didn't know Colleen was going to college."

Somebody drifts by and hands Jax a joint. One hit and he passes it toward me, but I wave it away.

"You sure? It's good shit."

"I'm cool."

He holds the smoke in but talks, anyway, in a high-pitched falsetto. "You're the dude with the thing on YouTube."

"Yeah, *High School Confidential*. Part of it, anyway."

He digs in a pocket and comes up with what has to be Beyond BlackBerry Supremo. His fingers dance across the keypad, and all of a sudden, there's Oliver.

Jax watches, barely chewing, washing everything down with beer, eyeing the brownies when he isn't looking at the little screen in his hand. Behind us, Randy yells, "What? What? A week ago you said two days."

"Bro," Jax says, tapping his phone, "this guy is gay."

"Yeah."

"Well, that shit is sick. Why put that sick shit on You-Tube? Little kids watch YouTube."

That pretty much propels me onto my feet. I find Colleen and say, "We're out of here."

"I know. You're right. I just want to get Luci on her feet."

"I'll be outside."

It's chilly on what I guess is the balcony, except it runs the length of the building. An outside hall, maybe. Anyway, I wish I'd worn a jacket. There's a deli across the street with a table and a big umbrella. Inside, all the lights are off except one. Under that, somebody is working on a computer. Working and not smoking dope.

I hear a door open. A woman holding a baby walks to the railing, talking on a cell phone. When she sees me, she turns her back.

Music leaks out of the apartment behind me. Hip-hop stuff. Thug life: get rich, go to jail, die.

A big black car stops right underneath me. I like the way the exhaust turns red when it curls past the taillights. I wish I had my camera.

Just then the door behind me opens and Colleen steps out. She shivers and leans into me. "What a fucking mistake this was," she says.

"Is Luci okay?"

"I leave her alone for one minute, she does a line of coke, and now she wants to dance on the table." She shudders and holds my arm with both hands. "What's on at the Rialto?" she asks.

"Creature Features."

"Let's go, okay?"

* * *

Colleen drives slowly, one hand on the wheel, the other on me. Every block or so, she shakes her head and swears under her breath. "What was I thinking?" she finally says out loud.

And I know she's not really looking for an answer.

We park across the street from the Rialto, next to the Blockbuster store, and wait till it's safe to cross. When the light changes and we reach the other curb, she stops. "This is where we met," she says.

"We met inside. We came out here afterward."

"But this is where I threw up."

"You threw up out the window of Grandma's Cadillac."

"It's all so romantic. We should come here every year on our anniversary."

We've missed Lon Chaney Jr. in *The Wolf Man,* but we're in time for *Creature from the Black Lagoon.*

Mrs. Stenzgarden has gone home. Reginald, the manager, sells us tickets at the door and chants, "'Not since the beginning of time has the world beheld a terror like this.'" Then he points to the poster where the Gill-Man cradles the lovely Kay.

"She's scared of him, right?" asks Colleen.

"Oh, yeah," Reginald says. "The monsters never get the girl."

"Poor fuckers." She nudges me. "Give me a couple of bucks, Ben. Since I don't get to smoke about a pound of hash, I'll settle for a Pepsi."

Reginald watches her walk away. "She's actually your girlfriend?" he asks.

"We met here," I tell him.

"No way."

"We're going to name our first man-child Rialto."

"Lucky you."

I watch him watch Colleen. "How's business?" I ask.

"Terrible. Too many DVDs, too much Netflix and movies on demand."

Colleen comes back, links her arm through mine. We're semi-alone. Reginald has to sell another latecomer a ticket. A few lost souls wander the shabby lobby.

She whispers, "That could be me on that bed at Amber's place."

"No, it couldn't. You're smarter than that."

"I'm not. I'm reckless and stupid." She kisses me like I'm about to leave for Afghanistan. "I'm going to call over there one more time, okay?" She points. "I'll just be, you know, in my office."

She glides toward the steps leading up to the balcony and sits down. While she talks, I peek inside. Thirty people, maybe, in the whole place. Some of them read. Most just stare at the huge screen, pristine and perfect as a field of snow.

Any minute now, that screen will be full of life. A beautiful girl, a handsome ichthyologist, a loathsome missing link with webbed hands and feet who can still fall in love.

Impulsively, I pull out my phone and call my mother. Who picks up.

"Mom? It's Ben. Your son, yes. I'm just . . . Colleen and I are at . . . She's here, but she's . . . Wait, she was just talking to somebody, but now . . . Sure."

Colleen whispers, "Amber took Luci home."

"Good." I hold the phone against my chest while I say, "She's my mother, but she wants you."

"Well, yeah," Colleen says. "Who'd want to talk to a resentful little crippled urchin boy?"

"Since you put it that way." I hand her the phone, and she takes a second to lean in and put her tongue in my ear, so that every drop of blood charges through my body.

"Delia," I hear her say, "what's happening in Azusa? I know it. Working just sucks. My feet are killing me, too."

I look at those dangerous shoes of hers, that little skirt holding on to her hips for dear life.

Just then the lights go off, on, off, on. Reginald still treats this place like it was a real theater. The lights are to warn his patrons that intermission is over.

I push back the heavy, dusty curtains and let a couple of people file by me. I look at Colleen, who stands up. I hear her say, "We'll talk tomorrow for sure, Delia, okay? I have to go now. The movie's about to start."

THE END